WILD TALENT

A Novel of the Supernatural

For Clint
with very best
wishes
Eileen

WILD TALENT

A Novel of the Supernatural

Eileen Kernaghan

EILEEN KERNAGHAN

Ucon 33

thistledown press

Thistledown Press Ltd.
633 Main Street
Saskatoon, Saskatchewan, S7H 0J8
www.thistledownpress.com

Library and Archives Canada Cataloguing in Publication
Kernaghan, Eileen
Wild talent : a novel of the supernatural / Eileen Kernaghan.
ISBN 978-1-897235-40-9
I. Title.
PS8571.E695W55 2008   C813'.54   C2008-904518-1

Publisher Cataloging-in-Publication Data (U.S.)
(Library of Congress Standards)
Kernaghan, Eileen.
Wild talent : a novel of the supernatural / Eileen Kernaghan.
[264] p. : cm.
Summary: The strange tale of a sixteen-year-old Scottish farm worker whose fear of being sentenced as a witch propels her to flee her home to London and the late 19th century world of spiritualists and theosophists, artists and esoteric cults.
ISBN: 978-1-897235-40-9 (pbk.)
1. Supernatural — Fiction. 2. Occult fiction. I. Title.
[Fic] dc22 PZ7.K45785Wil 2009

Cover photograph: *Woman in Yellow*, by Dante Gabriel Rossetti @ Tate, London, 2008
Cover and book design by Jackie Forrie
Printed and bound in Canada

10 9 8 7 6 5 4 3 2 1

Canada Council Conseil des Arts
for the Arts   du Canada

ARTS BOARD

Canadian   Patrimoine
Heritage   canadien

Thistledown Press gratefully acknowledges the financial assistance of the Canada Council for the Arts, the Saskatchewan Arts Board, and the Government of Canada through the Book Publishing Industry Development Program for its publishing program.

ACKNOWLEDGMENTS

A version of Chapter Six appeared as a short story, "Dinner with HPB", in *Crime Through Time III* (Berkley, 2000).

Many thanks to my indispensable first readers: my daughter Sue, my husband Pat, my friends Casey Wolf and Mary Choo, and members of the Helix speculative writing workshop; and very special thanks to Seán Virgo for his immensely helpful and perceptive editing.

For Edward Leander

I can't accept the reality of anything, in such an indeterminate existence as ours.
— Charles Fort, *Wild Talents*

THE BORDERS

. . . lost and helpless youngsters, under hard task-masters, in strange surroundings . . .
— Charles Fort, *Wild Talents*

CHAPTER ONE

March 2nd, 1888

My mother has sent me a gift of this journal, with roses and pansies on the cover, and a great many blank pages to be filled. And so tonight, now that my little cousins are asleep and I have an hour to myself, I mean to begin recording the story of my life. I will do my best to make it (as Miss Charlotte Brontë said of *Jane Eyre*) "a plain tale with few pretensions".

When I was younger and still in school I saw my life writ clear before me. A fine life it would be, with an oak desk in a big sunny room, windows looking out on a garden, bookshelves all round, and one long shelf of books that would have my own name, Jean Guthrie, in gold letters on their spines. I would not entertain visitors, for my time would be taken up by my work, but now and again I might take the train to Edinburgh where the university is, to attend a lecture. Or if I wished to meet with my publishers, as the Misses Brontë did, I might travel all the way to London, and there would be parties in my honour. I would order a Paris gown for such occasions — sober in colour, of dignified cut but very elegant.

It was my father taught me to love words, showed me the way they can be made to sing, to make patterns and images that linger in the mind long after the page is turned. If my father were here with me now, instead of in the kirkyard, it would break his heart, to see what has become of all his hopes for me. As it broke my heart to see him laid in the cold ground.

But I must begin at the beginning, for that is what Miss Brontë does. He was a scholar, my father, and meant for greater things than a village schoolmaster's post. That was the lot God gave him, and he accepted it with good grace, but for me he wanted the respect of learned folk that had never been accorded him. He would not spare himself, in work or in study, and it seemed to me, in the last year of his life, that all his frail strength was consumed by that restless mind.

Be that as it may, he left my mother with two bairns to care for, one still at the breast, and me, who was the oldest, the only one in our household fit for work.

Today I was up at 5:30, with cold mist curling over the fields, to be at the stables by first light. The steward set me to work sorting tatties for the spring planting: six in the morning till six at night stooped over the pit in a grey drizzle, up to my boot-tops in mud, my hands half-frozen in my gloves. And on this day — though it has passed as drearily as the ones before and the ones to follow — I am sixteen years old.

《 《 《

When I opened this journal, I found a letter tucked between the pages, in my mother's careful hand. "I think of you every day, dearest Jeannie. If only you did not have to live so many miles away! Still, what a blessing in disguise that your Uncle James had no daughter to hire out with him, and took you on instead. The life of a kitchen servant would never suit you — better far to be outdoors in the fresh air."

Well, she is right enough in that. I had no fondness for scrubbing pots and sweeping floors, and little aptitude for either one, as my mother has often enough observed. I thought that outdoor work would suit me better, and maybe it will if it stops raining and the north wind stops blowing, and summer ever comes. And if another steward of a more forgiving nature should be hired. And if my cousin George should fall into a ditch and drown. (That is a wicked thing to write, and I should scratch it out. But in this book, which none will ever read save myself, I mean to speak honestly and from the heart.)

That raw February morning when I went with my Uncle James to the hiring fair, I guessed well enough what my life was to become. I was not yet fourteen, shivering with cold and nerves in my thin jacket, while the farmers came by to ask my uncle, "Are ye to hire? And do you have a woman or girl with you?" Other women were laughing and chattering, in a holiday mood, for they'd not have a free day again before New Year's. And there was I, near dying of shame while the farmers looked me up and down, and my uncle swearing I was a braw strong girl, with back and arms meant for stooking sheaves and cleaning byres. No Paris gowns it was to be, for Jeannie Guthrie, but an apron and drugget skirt. No feathered chapeau, but a bondager's kerchief and wide straw hat ruched with red and black; no stockings of silk, but rough tweed leggings and tackety lace-up boots.

So then. Here I am, and here I must bide. And it is past time to blow the candle out.

CHAPTER TWO

Sunday, May 13

How could I let so many weeks slip by, and write nothing in my journal? Hell, as my father used to say (and Samuel Johnson before him) is paved with good intentions. But after these long days of planting and sowing and thistle-chopping, I fall into bed with scarce the energy to wash my face. And there is no rest on the wet days for then we must bide inside and sew the grain sacks. But now the real spring has come, the evenings grow longer, and I must use this precious hour of a Sunday dusk to say what has happened these weeks past.

But first I will write of what we did last night, Nellie Douglas and Edith Graham and I. It was a glorious spring evening, and we all went together to the dance in the village hall. I set out in a blithe enough frame of mind, excited to be away from the farm for a few hours, but my heart sank when I looked into the hall and saw that George was there. I remembered too many awkward encounters in byre and turnip shed, and when we met as we must in the eightsome reel, the look in his eye and the touch of his hands made my skin creep. The other girls think him handsome, even if they do not like him much. But Sally from the north, who is a sharp-tongued lass never caring what she says, told me once, "He's a randy wee man, your cousin George. I willna stand on a ladder near him, for fear he will look up my skirts." Rough spoken she may be, but Sally has the right of it. Though we are warned to keep clear of Irish harvesters, they are all talk and I can see no real harm in them. It is my cousin George I avoid whenever I can.

Still and all, we three were in a giddy mood as we made our way home under a clear sky, with moon and stars to light our path. Though Edith and Nellie are neither clever nor well-educated they are cheerful, good-hearted girls, and they never tease me, as George often does, for my bookish speech.

"I willna sleep," said Nellie, "I am that overwrought with the dancing." And Edith said, "Come home with me, my father will be long asleep" (for her mother is dead and she and her father live alone in their cottage). "It is nigh on midnight. Let's light a candle and look into the glass to see who we will marry."

"We need an apple for that," said Nellie.

"We have some keepers from my auntie's cellar," Edith said, and that decided us. And so like three mice we crept into her darkened cottage, with our hands over our mouths so as not to wake Edith's father, who was snoring in a corner of the downstairs room.

Edith lit a candle and fetched the apples from the cupboard — poor things too long stored and shrivelled to nothing, but with flesh enough still to make one bite. With no bairns in the family, Edith had the upper room to herself, and so with candle in hand she led us up the stairs, stepping carefully so the boards would not creak.

She found her looking glass and gave it to Nellie, saying. "You are the eldest, you must go first."

"Is it midnight? We canna do it before midnight."

"Dead on," said Edith, and she showed us her little clock. She handed Nellie one of the apples.

By candlelight, Nellie unplaited her long hair. Then she put out her hand for an apple. She took a single bite, spat out the chunk and tossed it over her left shoulder. "The comb — I must have the comb." Edith put it into her hand, and she drew it through her hair, all the while peering anxiously in the glass at the space over her left shoulder.

"Who do you see?" we whispered. "Do you see a face?"

"Oh aye, I see him right there over my shoulder, with such a come-hither look!"

"Who? Who?" we hissed at her.

She shot us a mischievous grin. "I do believe it is none other than Robin from the big house," and we all laughed, for she of course meant the heir to all this land, Mr. Murdoch's handsome elder son.

"Get away with you," said Edith. "You see no such thing. What would young Robin have to do with the likes of you? My turn now," and she took the glass from Nellie's hand. But when she had had her turn, she would not say who she had seen, only gave us a look like a cat in cream.

"Now you," she said, and handed me the glass.

I did just as the others, but hard though I stared, I could see no face but my own, and over my shoulder there was naught but darkness. I like to think it was because I have

yet to meet him, the Mr.Rochester to my Jane. But Nellie
says it means I will not marry at all.

❮ ❮ ❮

May 19

Where shall I begin? Everything has changed, and I cannot
bear to imagine what tomorrow may bring.

Ever since the dance there was no avoiding cousin
George. Everywhere I went on the farm, he was lying in
wait. I swear he would have crept up these stairs at night,
if not for fear of waking his sisters. This morning I was
mucking the byre and when I looked up there was he was,
lurking in the open doorway. As soon as I saw the grin on
his face I knew what he was after. He slammed shut the
barn door and started toward me. "A randy wee man," Sally
called him. He was no taller than I, but broad and strong,
and I knew I was no match for him.

I snatched up an empty milk bucket and hurled it at his
head. He ducked just in time.

"Why did you do that?"

"Let me be, or I will do it again, and I willna miss."

"Why so skittish, Jeannie Guthrie? It's only a kiss I'm
after — what's the harm in that?"

"George, we are cousins."

"What matter? Cousins marry."

"If you think I would marry you . . . "

He grinned, though truth to tell it was more of a smirk.

"Mebbe it wasnae the kirk I had in mind."

He moved closer, and I broke out in a cold sweat. There
was no way of escape, standing as he did between me and

the door. At that moment I spied a pitchfork leaning against a post; and at the same instant he reached for me.

And then all at once there was blood, and George was clutching his shoulder, and cursing in a shrill, outraged voice. The pitchfork, that a moment before had been standing harmlessly against the wall, was now lying at his feet. One of the tines had struck by his shoulder, piercing shirt and flesh.

He clutched his shoulder and stared at the blood welling up between his fingers. "You've killed me," he said, and there was a kind of puzzlement as well as anguish in his look.

"I haven't," I cried. "I didn't." Something had happened, sure enough, and George without question was wounded; yet I felt it had naught to do with me.

"You're a witch," he said, and what I saw in his face now was hatred, and bewilderment, and naked fear.

☾ ☾ ☾

They fetched George to the steward's cottage, and the steward's wife cleaned his wound and bound it up while they waited for the doctor to come from the village. If his wound should turn bad he may die, and then I will be a murderess, and must be taken away to prison, and will hang. Though perhaps — and I pray it be so — the wound is not a fatal one. Still, he named me a witch — though I swear what I did was through no conscious intent, but a thing I could not control. They burned witches once; and not so very long ago they threw them in the water to see if they would float or drown. I think there are folk hereabout who still hold to such beliefs.

And after all his wound may be deep, and may fester, and he will die. And I will hang for it.

There is naught for it, but to run away.

❰ ❰ ❰

Sunday, May 20

I have made a plan. Today out of shame I did not walk to the kirk with the others, but shut myself up in the cottage, and thought hard on what I must do. There are many ways my plan may go awry, but I can think of no better one. Even if George lives there is no place for me here, when I have impaled my cousin with a fork and have maybe been the death of him. I have made up my mind to go to London. I always meant to go there, though not so soon. No one knows me there, and I will change my name. I have a little money saved up from my wages that will pay for my railway ticket, and if I manage very carefully, a room for a week or two. There are publishers in London, and surely one will hire me, if only for some menial task. And whatever I earn I will send to my mother, save for what little I need for food and lodging.

I have packed my few books that were my father's; my good wool dress and my Sunday bonnet. My bondager's costume I will leave behind, all but my tackety boots, for it is a long walk across the fields to the station.

CHAPTER THREE

Monday, May 21

I t was not yet light when I crept out of the house, and I dared not take any food from the larder for fear of waking my aunt and uncle; and so as I made my way in the chill grey dawn toward Berwick I was hungry and thirsty and my spirits very low. But as I came near Berwick I could hear the dawn chorus of the birds, and then the sun rose. From the fields all around came the fragrance of dew-soaked grass, and in the hedgerows the hawthorn was in bloom. I was sorry, then, that I must leave. But I thought, however drab and grey the city may prove to be, and whatever misadventures may await me there, I cannot stay in a place where they think me at best a witch, at worst a murderess. And I remembered how Father used to say that opportunity could grow out of mischance, so as I trudged towards Berwick station I imagined the oak desk, the sunny room, the shelves of books with my name in gilt; and I began to walk faster, with a lighter heart.

So here I sit, on the morning train to London, with my journal on my lap. The woman beside me stared when I sat down, and I know how bedraggled I must look, with my hem all smirched and my boots muddy where I cut across the fields.

But now we have crossed the great viaduct, the Royal Border Bridge, that spans the Tweed from Berwick to Tweedmouth, and the train is gathering speed, hurtling into England. Stone walls and lonely farms and flocks of black-faced sheep all rush by, and on the other side is the sea, the Holy Isle of Lindisfarne, and the twin castles facing each other across the bay. Soon we will be in Newcastle, with the Borders and my old life forever behind me. I mean to keep a careful record of this journey, writ plain and in proper English, as a novelist would; for when I come to write the story of my life, this will be the opening chapter.

I must not think any more about George. It was a wicked thing I did, whether I meant it or not, and it is a shame I must live with. But more wicked than the act itself, I realize now, was the guilty joy I felt as my weapon found its mark.

LONDON

Adventure is my only reason for living.
— Alexandra David-Néel

...I am but the reflection of an unknown bright light... I cannot help myself that all these ideas have come into my brain, into the depth of my soul; I am sincere although perhaps I am wrong.
— Madame Helena Petrovna Blavatsky

CHAPTER FOUR

Tuesday, May 22.

M uch has happened.
     Only a few hours ago I was standing under the
clock tower of Kings Cross Station, gazing out in a panic at
the carriages and omnibuses rumbling along Euston Road.
In my haste to escape I had not considered how immense
London is, and how bewildering. Where should I spend
the night? There was a hotel next door, but it seemed
very grand and I knew I could not afford to stay there. I
thought I would ask some respectable lady where I might
find lodging, but there was such noise and confusion in
the station, with everyone so hurried and preoccupied,
that I quite lost my courage. And so I thought instead I
would look for something to eat, for I had had nothing since
Newcastle.

I bought a bun and a cup of tea and sat down on a bench
near a book stall. So tired I was, so frightened and so close
to tears, I could not think what I should do.

A young woman who was browsing at the book stall
happened to glance in my direction, and after a moment I

realized she was watching me with some curiosity. Presently she put down the book she was holding, and approached my bench. "Mademoiselle, you seem a little distressed. Is there anything I can do to help?"

She had a pleasant, open face and in her plain dark serge coat and skirt and sensible hat looked respectable enough, and so I took a chance and spoke to her. "Do you know where I might find an inexpensive rooming house?"

She glanced round at once, and replied, "*Mais oui*, I believe there are a great many such places around Kings Cross." I liked her clear French voice, with its lilting accent.

"Perhaps you could direct me . . ." I started to say, and felt my voice tremble so that I could not go on.

She looked at me with concern. "Mademoiselle, are you quite alone in London? Have you no friends or family you may go to?"

I shook my head. My eyes prickled, my throat had seized up. Tears ran down my face and I swiped at them with a gloved hand.

Calmly the young woman produced a handkerchief.

"This will not do," she said, as I dabbed at my eyes. "Come, there is a public house just over there with a private ladies' room in the back. We can sit and talk, and have some supper if you wish."

The thought of supper cheered me a little. I nodded, and she took my arm in friendly fashion. She was slender and not very tall — her head came only to my shoulder — but she carried herself like a duchess. So much at ease she seemed, with such an air of confidence, that I imagined her much older than myself; though as I now know, she is only twenty.

As we came out of the station a young girl approached us. She could not have been more than ten years old. Her small, pinched face had a sickly pallor, and there were dark circles under her eyes. She wore a draggled, shapeless garment that trailed behind her through the dust. My companion paid her no heed; but when this poor creature confronted me with a grimy hand outstretched, I thought how easily this could be my own fate; and so I gave her tuppence I could ill afford.

When we had crossed the busy street and settled ourselves in the small private room at the back of the public house, my new acquaintance ordered hot soup and some bread and cheese, and over my protests, insisted on paying.

"So then," she said. "First things first. You have not told me your name."

It was on the tip of my tongue to say "Jeannie". Then I thought, this is the beginning of my new life. "Jean," I told her. "My name is Jean Guthrie."

"And I am Alexandra David." She pronounced her surname in the French way, `Dahveed'.

"Now then, Jeanne." I liked the way she softened the hard 'J' of my name. "As to the question of a lodging place. I fear you will find the rooming houses round here quite unsuitable. No, do not look so forlorn — I have a suggestion. At the house where I am lodging, I believe there is presently one room unoccupied."

What good fortune, this happenstance meeting!

"It is very pleasant," continued Mlle David. "Quite cheap and very conveniently situated, close to the British Museum. While the food leaves something to be desired, one's fellow lodgers are intriguing. Best of all, one is left to oneself and can come and go as one pleases."

I thought of my old life under the watchful eyes of my aunt and uncle, in a cottage too cramped to afford any privacy. To be left to oneself, to come and go as one liked — what an excellent arrangement!

"But if I am to recommend you as a lodger, you must first tell me a little about yourself. What can have brought you to London, quite unchaperoned and so clearly in distress?"

What could I tell her? I could not speak of what George had hoped to do to me; nor could I tell her of the terrible thing I had done to George. And so I stumbled through an explanation, describing the ill fortune which had befallen my family and the hard life I had led as a bondager, with no hope of ever improving my lot. "Also," I told her, feeling myself blush, "there was a cousin who wished to marry me."

It was, I suppose, not so very far from the truth.

"And you did not like him, and so you have run away."

"Yes. And I know it was a very foolish thing to do."

To my surprise, she burst out laughing. "*Au contraire,* it was entirely sensible. I myself have run away more times than I can count."

I stared at her. "You have?"

"Indeed." She smiled in recollection. "The first time, I was five. My family was moving from Paris, which I loved, to Brussels, which I knew I would hate. And so the day before we left, I slipped away from my nanny in the Bois de Vincennes. A gendarme caught me, and took me to the police station." She added cheerfully, "I scratched him. I was *une petite sauvage.*" Pouring us each another cup of tea, she went on, "I ran away from Brussels too. I walked to Holland, and then I took a ferry boat to England. I would have stayed, if my money had not run out. And then when I was seventeen I took an umbrella and a copy of Epictetus's *Maxims*, and hiked over the Alps to Italy. My mother had to come and fetch me from Milan."

"But were you, too, running away from an unsuitable marriage?" In novels I have read, young women generally undertake such exploits for reasons of the heart. And though she is not especially beautiful, with her luminous dark eyes and fine complexion, and her look of lively intelligence, Mlle David must surely not have lacked for suitors.

She laughed. *"Mais non,* what an idea! I do not think about men — they are more trouble than they are worth!"

I have found a soulmate, I decided.

"Now then," she said, "if you are quite finished your tea, we will go to the house of the Supreme Gnosis. For tonight you will be my guest, and tomorrow I will ask my patroness Madame Morgan to sponsor your membership as well."

"The Supreme Gnosis — what a peculiar name for a lodging house!"

"No more peculiar," said Alexandra, "than the members. But you will discover that for yourself."

"But surely," I protested, "to become a member . . . . there must be initiations, qualifications . . . "

"Non, non, there is no difficulty," said Mlle David. "The Supreme Gnosis is no secret society, merely a community of people who wish to study eastern religions and philosophies. To join, it is only necessary to share that purpose."

I wondered what my staunch Presbyterian mother would think of that. But my father surely would have approved. "Gnosis" means "knowledge", and had he not encouraged me in all manner of scholarly pursuits?

And so we hired a hansom cab from the ranks parked outside the station, and we clattered off in the fading light along the Euston Road.

Thus Mlle David, like a guardian angel, has brought me to safe haven. I am too weary to write more. But tomorrow I will describe what a *very* peculiar place is the house of the Supreme Gnosis

❮ ❮ ❮

Wednesday, May 23

My room is large, though not so large as Alexandra's, and amply furnished. Besides my bed I have a wardrobe, writing desk, dressing table, and three chairs, two straight and one upholstered. There is also an electric lamp with a flowered glass shade and a brass pull-chain. The society is quite up to date in its domestic arrangements. And this morning when I drew back the curtains from the tall windows, I looked out into a small, well-kept garden.

Perhaps the home of the Supreme Gnosis is no different from any well-appointed London house. And yet there is a certain mystery about this place that fills me with a vague unease. Alexandra says she feels it too, and has added to my disquiet with tales of vibrating doors, and ghostly processions circling her bed. Perhaps she is only inventing these stories to frighten me for her own entertainment. But it is not wise to dwell on them at night, when I am alone. Even now, as I write, I feel a shiver down my spine — wondering if I will wake in darkness to find those vaporous figures hovering around my bed. Alexandra keeps her lamp lit while she sleeps. I intend to do the same.

But even more eccentric are the inhabitants of this house. I wondered at their gaunt appearance, till I saw how little they eat. A maid awoke me this morning at seven with tea and biscuits, and I thought, what luxury. But the tea was weak as dishwater, and breakfast, when I came downstairs, was still more disappointing — some nuts, a thin unsalted gruel, and more dry biscuits. I longed for the bowls of thick porridge that broke our weekday fast on the farm, still more for the fried bread and ham we had on Sundays. Tea this afternoon was a further disappointment — sconeless, butterless and jamless.

Alexandra says that when she complained about the sparseness of the food, she was sternly advised that the president of the Supreme Gnosis existed on a dozen almonds a day, and now and again an orange.

I am writing this in the library, and trying not to think about food. It's a large, warm, comfortable room, dim and fragrant with incense smoke. The members of the Society — Gnostics, I suppose they are called — wander in and out in long white robes like half starved ghosts. They puff on cigarettes while they consult the books on alchemy, metaphysics and astrology that line the shelves.

I fancied myself well educated, because I have some French and Latin and a little Greek. But the subjects on which these Gnostics expound over their boiled cabbage and watery stew are far beyond my comprehension. However, Alexandra (she insists on my calling her that) can hold her own with the most erudite of our fellow lodgers. In fact, she is so clever and so well-read that I am quite in awe of her. She spends most her days in the library of the British Museum, and tells me she is planning to master Sanskrit and Tibetan. The books on her bedside table — the Ramayana, the Rig Vedas, the Koran — are none that I remember seeing in my father's library.

For all that, she seems a sensible young woman, and she often makes fun of the Gnostics, calling them "the extravagants". When we are alone she laughs at their talk of invisible beings they call the "Instructors" who descend from a high plane to impart their wisdom. "You must be careful in the library where you choose to sit," she warned me with a giggle, "or you may find yourself on an Instructor's lap!"

Alexandra says that when she first read the journals of the Society, which her friend Mrs. Morgan sent to her in Paris, she said *"Ces gens-là sont fous!"* Since then she has learned more respect for the Gnostics, who seek after knowledge as passionately as herself. She no longer thinks that they are mad. In this house, living among believers, one cannot ignore the shadowy presence of the spirit world.

But in the meantime, there are pressing matters in the material world I must attend to. Once I have paid for my lodging, my small hoard of money will be almost gone. Alexandra has offered to pay me to tutor her in English, but I know that is only out of charity, for her grasp of the language is very good. Somehow I must find work.

When I told Alexandra that I hoped to find a starting position with a publisher, or perhaps employment in a bookshop, her look was discouraging. "But you have no experience," she said, "and no letters of reference. Besides, they seldom hire women. Let us be practical. What useful skills do you possess? Needlework, perhaps?"

I shook my head. "My mother tried to teach me, but I could never make the stitches fine enough. Alexandra, if I am not to use my writing and my knowledge of books, then what skills have I to offer? Hoeing, thinning turnips, mending sacks?"

Alexandra's mouth twitched with laughter. "I fear there is little call in London, just now, for turnip-thinners." Then, more soberly: "But you are not without education. Perhaps you could seek a position as governess?"

I thought of Jane Eyre, and how she had come to meet her Mr. Rochester at Thornfield Hall. Though a teacher's life was not what I had planned, there was merit to the idea. Then Alexandra, having second thoughts, pointed out that a governess should be qualified to teach not only mathematics, geography, natural science, the classical and romance languages — but also music, dancing (proper dancing, not the country sort), etiquette and deportment. Needless to say, in these latter disciplines I am sadly lacking.

Alexandra must have sensed my despair, for she said, "Be of good heart, *ma petite*. We will think of something."

That she called me her little one, when I was so much taller than she, made me smile, and I felt a little better.

"Quite possibly," said Alexandra reassuringly (though not, I thought, with much conviction) "some family of limited means with clever sons, and no daughters in need of dancing lessons, would be happy to employ you. We will place an advertisement in the newspaper, and I will help you to compose it."

CHAPTER FIVE

Wednesday June 6

A fortnight has gone by, and there have been no replies to my advertisement. Alexandra has lent me money to pay for another week's lodging, but I have naught to send home to my mother, and I must quickly find employment. I am strong and healthy, and well accustomed to hard work. There are factories in London where I could apply, or if all else fails, I could hire out as a charwoman or a scullery maid. But Alexandra will not hear of this. She says that I have too good a mind to waste it in menial labour. Of course I am flattered that she thinks me clever, but cleverness will avail me little if I cannot earn my keep.

Thursday, June 7.

An acquaintance at the British Museum has told Alexandra of a London book-bindery employing women. The work sounds pleasant, and if I am not to be hired by a publisher, at least I would have a small part in the making of books. I mean to apply on Monday. One of the Gnostic ladies has offered to lend me a skirt and shirtwaist, and Alexandra has said she will do my hair (she threatens to cut me a fringe) so that I will appear respectable. But I despair of my hands, so calloused and rough from outdoor work that no emollient will smooth them. And I must remember, when answering questions, not to fall into the broad Borders speech.

In the meantime, Alexandra and I have had a visitor. Our sponsor Mrs. Elisabeth Morgan came to call this afternoon, saying it was time she met her newest protégé. She is a lady of middle years, with a kind face and pleasant manner, though it seems to me rather eccentric in her dress. This afternoon she wore a long plum-coloured velvet waistcoat over a grey woollen gown belted with a tasselled cord and over that a paisley shawl. Perhaps this is a new London fashion, though she did put me in mind a little of the White Queen in Alice.

Of course Alexandra has not told her why I came to London and Mrs. Morgan was too discreet to inquire, though when I said that I had been a bondager, she gazed at me admiringly through the monocle she carries on a ribbon. "To have led such a hard life, and yet still aspire to cultivate the spirit and the intellect — my dear child, you make me feel quite humbled." Clearly, Mrs. Morgan is persuaded that I, like Alexandra, am a seeker after arcane wisdom. I spoke as little as possible, for fear of revealing my true ignorance; leaving Alexandra to seize the reins of the conversation in her usual confident way.

"It is time, my dear Alexandra," said Mrs. Morgan, setting down her teacup, "that you paid your respects at 17 Lansdowne Road. You must join our little gathering this Saturday, and of course Miss Guthrie must come as well."

So saying, she opened her reticule and produced a printed card.

It was an invitation, which Alexandra read aloud.

"Madame Blavatsky. At Home, Saturday 4:00 to 10:00 o'clock."

"This Madame Blavatsky," said Alexandra. "They say she is *très formidable*."

"Indeed she is," said Elisabeth Morgan. "But my dear, you must not let her intimidate you. You too can be *très formidable*!"

Of this Madame Blavatsky, I know only what Alexandra has told me: that she is widely read and widely travelled, and a famous Theosophist. 17 Lansdowne Road, it seems, is the very epicentre of London occultism. I have no notion what a Theosophist might be, and I look forward to Saturday with some trepidation. Still, as Alexandra says, it should prove *"bien intéressant."*

CHAPTER SIX

Sunday, June 10

Yesterday was the strangest day I have ever spent; and I suspect there may be stranger still to come.

Mrs. Morgan came to collect us in late afternoon, and we travelled by cab to Holland Park. So far I had seen little of London. As we made our way though the crowded, noisy streets in the shadow of enormous buildings, with never a chink or cranny where green things might grow, it seemed to me like a city so vast it had swallowed up the world. I thought I would never wish to find myself afoot here, and alone. But Lansdowne Road was pleasant enough — a broad street of very large stone houses (villas, Mrs. Morgan calls them) set among clipped trees and shrubbery, each one with its tidy garden.

Just after six we drew up at Number 17, which overlooks the park. The house seemed very grand, and I was anxious about our costumes, for we had no afternoon frocks or feathered hats, only our workaday serge. Alexandra, who is of independent mind and I suspect may have anarchist leanings, clearly had not given this much thought. Kind

Mrs. Morgan, in flowing dove-grey silk, tried to reassure me, saying, "My dear, Madame Blavatsky has never been one to concern herself with fashion!"

But the woman who answered our knock seemed to me the very epitome of fashion, a slender lady of fifty or so in a flounced and beaded dinner gown, her ash-blonde hair immaculately coiffed.

"Mrs. Morgan, do come in, how pleasant to see you again!"

"My dear Countess," said Mrs. Morgan, as we all stepped into the entrance-hall, "may I present my young protégé, Mlle Alexandra David, and her friend Miss Guthrie. My dears, this is the Countess Constance Wachmeister, who looks after this household with quite miraculous efficiency."

"HPB is in her office," said the Countess. Her competent, take-charge manner seemed quite at odds with her gown. "She has especially asked to meet the young ladies."

"Courage, my dears," said Mrs. Morgan, *sotto voce*, as the Countess led us away. I looked at Alexandra in alarm.

Madame Blavatsky awaited us in her ground-floor study, seated in a great armchair with her back to a large and extraordinarily cluttered desk. Behind her, a bay window with half-drawn curtains looked out into the shadowy park. Every shelf and table was heaped with books, and more volumes were stacked haphazardly on the floor. Scattered about, as well, were all manner of exotic objects — oriental sculptures, Indian mats and wall-plaques, a golden Buddha. A gas stove glowed in a corner, filling the room with fusty warmth, and the close air held a lingering odour, sweet and cloying. (Alexandra whispered to me, afterwards, that it was hashish, which she had lately learned to recognise.) On one wall, looking curiously out of place, was a Swiss cuckoo clock. Though it seemed to be broken — for its weights were lying on the floor — as we sat down it gave a curious kind of sigh, or groan.

Madame Blavatsky herself was a huge, shapeless presence draped in a baggy black gown girdled with a black rope, the hem riding up to reveal grotesquely swollen ankles and feet. Her crinkly grey hair was pulled back into an untidy knot, her massive double-chinned face netted with wrinkles and yellow-tinged. Yet what one notices first is not that awkward bulk, but her large, luminous eyes. A piercing azure-blue, they are filled with a shrewd intelligence. They seem to transfix you, so that you cannot look away.

"Here is the young lady from Belgium," said the Countess, "and her Scottish friend." And with that she abandoned us to Madame Blavatsky's mercies.

"Where exactly in Belgium?" With nicotine-stained fingers Madame Blavatsky tapped a cigarette into an overflowing ashtray.

"From Brussels, Madame. But I was born in Paris, and lived there until I was five."

"Paris," said Madame Blavatsky, with a look of distaste. "I understand they are ruining the view with some sort of enormous metal excrescence."

"Monsieur Eiffel's tower," said Alexandra. "Indeed," she added, in her correct but hesitant English, "it is the centre of much controversy. There are those who call it *'Notre Dame des ferrailleurs'*."

"The junkman's Notre Dame — exactly so," said Madame B. "Well then, Mademoiselle David. Mrs. Morgan tells me you are a student of the occult."

Alexandra seemed to recoil a little under the intensity of that bright blue gaze. "It interests me a great deal, that is true."

"And you plan to make it your career?"

"*Au contraire*," said Alexandra. "I have trained for a career in music — but now I believe I would like to study medicine, and perhaps become a medical missionary." Devious Alexandra! I knew she was really in London to escape from her dreary Brussels home.

"A doctor — now there is a worthy undertaking!"

"It's difficult, of course, for a woman . . . " Alexandra started to say.

"Flapdoodle!" said Madame Blavatsky, fiercely. "These days a woman can do anything she wishes. I myself am a living example of that. Did you know that I fought with Garibaldi's army at the Battle of Mentana, and was wounded five times, and left for dead in a ditch?"

"*Incroyable!*" murmured Alexandra. (We had already heard this tale from Elisabeth Morgan.)

"And furthermore I had a dear friend, Anna Kingsford, who was an eminent doctor. It doesn't do to limit one's aspirations."

Though she had yet to address a word to me, I felt myself warming to this immense, untidy, blunt-spoken woman.

"When you have finished your medical studies," said Madame Blavatsky, "you must come and see me again. By then my good Dr. Mennell will have retired, and perhaps I will take you on as my personal physician. That is, if these rotting kidneys have not already finished me off."

"I had thought," said Alexandra politely, "that I might use my skills in the Orient. Even perhaps Tibet."

"Ah, yes," said Madame B. with sudden animation. "I myself have travelled extensively in the Forbidden Kingdom."

Alexandra said nothing. I think, like me, she was trying to imagine those elephantine lower limbs transporting their owner over the Himalayas.

But now Madame B. turned the full force of her attention on me. "And you will be the young person from Scotland. A backward country, in many respects, though I'm told it produces excellent doctors. Are you also a medical student?"

I summoned my courage and prayed not to trip over my tongue. "No, Madame. I have hopes of one day becoming an author."

"Hah!" said Madame B. "Everybody wants to be an author. Better you should take in laundry, or scrub floors for a living. It's easier work." She stubbed out her cigarette, and paused in the act of reaching for another. "There is the dinner-bell. We must see what guests have come to amuse us tonight. Let me have your arm. These gouty old legs of mine are giving me no end of trouble." So saying, she heaved herself to her feet, and leaning heavily on my shoulder she began her laborious progress into dinner.

We went through folding doors into the dining room, where in the glow of gaslight a dozen or so guests were preparing to sit down to a meal.

The ladies, for the most part, were beautifully dressed in what I believe must be the latest fashion: loose, diaphanous tea-gowns; draped Grecian costumes lavishly embroidered with gold thread; and stayless, high-waisted gowns like the ones the actress Sarah Bernhardt wears. In my black serge skirt and high-collared white blouse, I was like a pigeon strayed into a flock of macaws. But when Alexandra pointed out one woman in a plain skirt and jacket and sturdy laced-up boots, with a red kerchief round her neck, I felt not so entirely out of place.

The evening, already odd, was to grow odder still. Madame Blavatsky settled herself at the head of table, ashtray at hand, and immediately launched into a sort of lecture. "The whole universe is filled with spirits," she declaimed loudly. "It's nonsense to believe that we are the only intelligent beings in the world. I believe there is latent spirit in all matter."

Mrs. Morgan, who was listening intently, turned to us with an encouraging smile. "Do join us, my dears," she said. We found two empty places and sat down.

The table was set for twenty at least, and people continued to arrive without ceremony in the middle of the soup course. They would find an empty chair, chat for a while, and then leave without waiting for the pudding. A perspiring housemaid appeared from time to time to set out more food and change the plates. It all seemed quite slapdash, and not at all like dinner parties in novels I have read.

I recognised none of the dishes we were served, but all seemed delicious, the more so because the Gnostics' fare had left me ravenous. However, I do not think that Borders folk would approve of Madame Blavatsky's table, for everything was strangely spiced, and there was not a scrap of mutton or mince or boiling beef to be seen.

Madame B. had begun to lecture again, her voice gaining steadily in volume as she warmed to her subject. "It's been recorded that some patients suffering from nervous diseases have been raised from their beds by a mysterious power, and it has been impossible to force them down. Thus we see that there is no such thing as the law of gravitation, as it's generally understood."

Some guests were moving closer to Madame Blavatsky and leaning forward so as not to miss a word. Others were drifting to the farther end. All this changing of places was a little like Mr. Dodgson's Mad Tea Party. Alexandra, who a moment earlier was deep in conversation with a pale, intense young poet, now had an older lady claiming her attention. (This was Lady Wilde, Alexandra told me later — the mother of the celebrated playwright. Lady Wilde seemed under the illusion that she was attending a séance.)

The lean, bespectacled gentleman on my right introduced himself as Charles Barker, a lecturer in zoology at Cambridge.

"Do try this lentil stew," he said, as he helped himself from the tureen. "You'll find it excellent. Though of course this vegetarianism is simply another of HPB's frauds. The woman is Russian, after all. She was raised on sausage and smoked goose."

As I tried to think how to answer, I heard from somewhere in mid-air the silvery chiming of a bell, and a long-stemmed red rose plummeted onto the table next to my wine-glass. I stared up at the ceiling.

"Aha," said Mr. Barker, sounding amused. "HPB is up to her parlour tricks again. Doesn't she realize we're all thoroughly bored by them?"

I pushed the rose nervously to one side, just in time to see a plain white envelope fall with a small thud onto my plate. I thrust my chair back from the table in alarm. Madame Blavatsky, who had ignored the mysterious chimes and the apparently heaven-sent rose, looked straight down the table at me, and smiled expansively.

"Look," she said in her hoarse smoker's voice. "The Mahatma has sent our young guest a letter. You must open it and read it to us, Miss Guthrie."

How awful to be suddenly the centre of everyone's attention! I'm sure I was blushing as I fumbled open the envelope. Inside was a sheet of a shell-pink writing paper with a message in heavy black ink: "To Miss Jean Guthrie. Master Koot Hoomi Singh sends a warm welcome to the young visitor from Scotland." The black letters were hastily scrawled, and there was a large inkblot in one corner. Where the signature should have been, there was a line of writing in some foreign script.

Alexandra, eager to see what was happening, had moved into the chair on my left. Wordlessly, I held out the paper for her to read.

"You should feel honoured, Miss Guthrie," said Charles Barker. "You hold in your hand one of the famous — or should I say infamous — Mahatma letters. According to HPB they are written somewhere in the Himalayas by a mysterious holy man, an initiate of the Brotherhood of the Snowy Range. And delivered, as you observe, by disembodied spirits — the astral post office, if you will."

"But what utter nonsense!" Alexandra burst out.

"Quite so," said Mr. Barker. "But you would be astounded, mademoiselle, at how many otherwise sensible people have been duped into believing this Mahatma is real."

Alexandra was examining the signature. "I believe this writing is Tibetan," she said.

"And do you read Tibetan, mademoiselle?" This was from a tall, fair-haired young man who had just joined us.

"Not at the moment. But I mean to study it, quite soon."

"Then, mademoiselle," said the young man, "you could be a valuable addition to our Society."

"Allow me to introduce Thomas Grenville-Smith," said Mr. Barker. "He is a colleague of mine at Cambridge."

Mr. Grenville-Smith solemnly shook hands with us, each in turn.

"Do you refer to the Theosophical Society?" asked Alexandra.

"Most definitely not," said the young man. "Dr. Barker and I are members of the Society for Psychical Research."

"Or the Spookical Research Society, as HPB would have it," said Charles Barker, holding up his wine-glass to be refilled.

"And what is that?"

"We are a group of likeminded scientists and scholars, dedicated to investigating paranormal phenomena."

"In other words, spooks," said Thomas Grenville-Smith. He looked over at me and smiled. It was an engaging smile, clearly meant to put me at ease, and I couldn't help but return it. Perhaps he understood how lost I felt in those strange surroundings, and how little a part of the conversation.

"I should explain," said Charles Barker, "that we are here to research Madame Blavatsky's psychic abilities."

"And what has your research shown?" asked Alexandra.

"So far we have reached no firm conclusions. However — " he dropped his voice and leaned in confidentially — "as you may have guessed, we are very much inclined to think she is a fraud."

"*Vraiment*!" exclaimed Alexandra. "On what grounds?"

"My dear young lady, one scarcely knows where to begin. Her entire history is a series of exaggerations and falsehoods and outrageous behaviour. Take, for example, these letters she insists are written by her "Tibetan Masters" — blatant forgeries, according to the report prepared for our society by Mr. Richard Hodgson, who travelled to India to investigate her claims. In fact, he suspects she may be a Russian spy."

I stole a glance along the table, to where Madame Blavatsky was still vigorously holding court. Slow-moving and cumbersome as she was, she seemed an unlikely sort of spy. And for all her outrageousness, I could not find it in my heart to dislike her. I have known women in the turnip-fields as rough-tongued and outspoken, and liked them the better for it. There was something about that fierce and penetrating blue gaze that made me hope she was not, after all, a fraud. And yet these were men of science, who spoke from scholarly evidence. And how much easier, after all, to believe that magically descending roses and letters from the spirit world were naught but sleight of hand.

"Certainly," continued Mr. Barker, "she has been shown to be a plagiarist. It seems that in this book of hers, *Isis Unveiled*, there are some two thousand passages copied without credit from other peoples' books. Richard Hodgson describes her in his report at one of the most accomplished and ingenious imposters in history."

"And one of the most interesting," said his companion Mr. Grenville-Smith. "Let us not forget that."

"Indeed yes," said Charles Barker. "Why else would we so determinedly pursue these investigations? But Mlle David, Miss Guthrie, I must warn you, she is a woman of forceful personality, and it is all too easy to fall under her spell."

As surely Mrs. Morgan has, I thought, for our sponsor had taken a seat near the head of the table, and was listening to Madame Blavatsky with the rapt expression of a devotee.

Just then Madame B. broke off her lecture and reached for a glass of water. Her gaze, as she set down her glass, moved along the table and came to rest on the two gentlemen from Cambridge. Quietly amused and faintly mocking, that look made it clear she was aware of every word they had said.

While Madame Blavatsky applied her full attention to her meal, Mrs. Morgan turned to her neighbour on the left, a gentleman with a clipped beard and long, curving moustache. Shortly thereafter she came to join us at our end of the table.

"Miss Guthrie," she said, "I have had a most interesting conversation with Madame Blavatsky's private secretary, Mr. Mead. He tells me that the members of the Lodge are quite overwhelmed with the work of preparing her new book for publication, on top of putting out a magazine and running a publishing company. They are sorely in need of another pair of hands. Of course I immediately thought of you."

I could only stare at her, she had taken me so much by surprise. But after I had a moment to reflect, I asked, "What would I be required to do?"

"Oh, I imagine file, sort papers, copy out information, run errands, that sort of thing. You can write in a good clear hand, can you not? And spell, and punctuate correctly?"

I nodded.

"Well then, as I understand the position, you are more than qualified. I will speak to Mr. Mead at once."

And it was as quick as that, and as easy. It seems that on the strength of Mrs. Morgan's recommendation, I have been offered employment at 17 Lansdowne Road. I am apprehensive, needless to say, but excited as well. The pay is not much — a few shillings a week — but I am to be given room and board, so it will cost me nothing to live. Now at last I will have a little money to send home. And how proud my father would be, to know that I have found a place, however humble, in the company of poets and scholars, and publishers of learned books.

CHAPTER SEVEN

June 17

I have not yet described the other inhabitants of 17 Lansdowne Road.

First of all, there are the two Messrs. Keightley, Archibald and Bertram. They are very alike, with beards and spectacles that give them a grave and scholarly look, though I think that neither is much above thirty years of age. Archibald is a doctor, Bertram a lawyer.

There is also Mr. Mead, a colonel's son, who I'm told was once a mathematician, but now has taken up Hindu philosophy. His name is George, and I wish it were not, for each time I hear Madame Blavatsky address him by his Christian name it gives me a start. But Mr. Mead, who is a kind and courteous gentleman, is as unlike that other George as I could wish anyone to be.

These, besides the Countess and myself, are the members of the household, each of us dedicated to the publication of the Great Work, and to the comfort and well-being of Madame Helena Petrovna Blavatsky — whom everyone calls HPB.

There is also a Mr. Fawcett who comes in to assist with the editing. As to visitors, they are many, and though formal visiting hours have been arranged, they are nonetheless apt to arrive in early afternoon and stay till midnight.

There is Mr. Willie Wilde, who is a journalist; his mother Lady Wilde, whom I have mentioned; and his sister-in-law Constance, who is the wife of Mr. Oscar Wilde the playwright.

Mr. Yeats is a frequent visitor, and has a tendency to monopolize the conversation. He seems to be a special favourite of HPB. She will not permit anyone to reprove him for talking too much, because she says he is a poet and therefore sensitive.

Madame Blavatsky is very regular in her hours. She is at her desk from six in the morning till six at night, preparing her new book *The Secret Doctrine: The Synthesis of Science, Religion and Philosophy* for publication. As I understand it (and certainly I do not understand it very well) it is about how the universe was created, and how the human race evolved over hundreds of millions of years until the present day. We are still working on Volume I, *Cosmogenesis*, which begins in Eternal Night when time and matter did not exist.

The Keightleys, who are retyping this enormous work, tell me they often despair of seeing it in print. When they first undertook the task they were confronted with an entirely disorganized pile of manuscript pages three feet high. Between them they have attempted to impose order upon chaos, but they admit the work would go much faster if HPB did not decide to alter the pages at the very moment they are to go to the printer.

One of Mr. Bertram's tasks is to check the many scholarly quotations. But the right books are never in the house, and must be sought out with great effort at the British Museum or elsewhere. Besides, HPB's page numbers are often written the wrong way round. She explains that she does not work from actual books, but from visions of books sent by the Tibetan Masters, which pass mysteriously before her eyes; and numbers in Astral Visions are apt to be reversed. I know that the gentlemen from the Psychical Research Society would scoff at this; but it is hard to imagine any more rational explanation, since she possesses so few of the books from which she quotes. Stranger still, the manuscript contains many complicated mathematical formulae, when it is clear that Madame B. does not understand mathematics at all. (She once said to the Countess's niece, "Could you tell me what is a pi?")

She is forever interrupting Mr. Bertram's work to make him search for some misplaced reference book or missing note. When these are not to be found, she flies into a great temper and accuses Mr. Bertram of being slipshod and incompetent. There is a story one of the visitors, Mr. Johnston, told me, that happened before the household moved to Lansdowne Road. One afternoon Mr.Johnston had been invited to tea, and while they were eating their toast and eggs HPB bellowed at Mr. Bertram that he was "greedy, idle, untidy, unmethodical and generally worthless." When the poor man tried to defend himself, she told him that he was "born a flapdoodle, lived a flapdoodle, and would die a flapdoodle." Mr. Bertram was so upset that his fork flew out of his hand and splattered egg yolk all across the tablecloth; and then he bolted out of the room.

At first I could not think how he could stand to be treated like this, when he is not even paid for his work. But now I have come to realize that as a Theosophist he is utterly dedicated to the publication of this great work, and so will put up with any amount of abuse.

I am resolved, when I become an author, to work in a more orderly fashion, and to treat my associates with greater respect. In the meantime I am at everyone's beck and call. I believe Mrs. Morgan envisioned me as an assistant to Mr. Mead, but in fact I am little more than a maidservant, employed to fetch and carry. I bring Madame B. the medicine for her heart, and a fresh supply of Turkish tobacco for her cigarettes, and a shawl to put round her shoulders, and I empty the ashtray on her desk when it overflows with half-smoked ends. Sometimes, though, I am asked to help proof-read and double-check quotations, and so I feel that I am playing a part, however small, in this vast enterprise.

❰ ❰ ❰

London, June 17.

I have written and thrown into the fire half a dozen letters to my mother. It is so difficult to know what to write. Words have deserted me, and my head is pounding. This last draft will have to do. Tomorrow I will write out a fair copy and put it in the mail, leaving off the return address. (Though even so, I worry that the police may find some way to trace me.)

Dearest Mother,

By now I expect you will have heard from Uncle James of my disappearance. I know how very worried you must be, and I hope you will find it in your heart to forgive me. If Uncle James has told you the circumstances of my departure, then you will understand why I had no choice but to leave.

You will be glad to know that I have found employment in a respectable household, so you need have no fears on my behalf. I will send money as soon as I am able.

Please kiss the bairns for me, and tell them they are always in my thoughts, as are you also. I promise I will write again very soon.

Your loving daughter,
Jeannie

CHAPTER EIGHT

June 26

On Sunday I went to visit Alexandra. She seemed to me a
little pale and subdued. When I asked after her health, she
told me, "I am well enough, but I have had a very curious
adventure."

One of the guests presently staying at the house of the
Supreme Gnosis is a landscape artist from Paris, called M.
Jacques Villemain. Alexandra seems quite smitten, although
of course she will not admit to this. She describes him as a
tall, pale, rather solemn young man with an unworldly air,
not at all like an *artiste parisien*. He is *très sérieux*, she
says. "I cannot imagine him dressed up in a costume at the
Beaux Arts Ball."

He was a mystic, he informed Alexandra, though not
religious, and he invited Alexandra to his room so that she
could see some of his work. His landscapes, he said, had a
secret reality that ordinary people could not perceive. Of
course Alexandra, who is insatiably curious, was intrigued;
though she did not think the English would approve of
her visiting a young man alone in his room. However,

he reassured her, saying that the adepts of the Supreme Gnosis regarded such conventions as absurd and in any case, all Gnostics were pure in spirit. "Besides," he said in all seriousness, "I will leave the door ajar" — which made Alexandra laugh.

All she saw at first were simple landscapes. "They seemed accomplished enough, with a certain charm, though whether they were anything out of the ordinary I was not qualified to judge. But Monsieur Villemain urged me to look deeper, and gradually I began to see the paintings with different eyes. It was, as he said, as though another, stranger reality hovered just beneath the surface."

Everywhere Alexandra looked — at rocks, flowers, bushes, mountains — she saw an unsettling double image. In one painting a vast deserted heath stretched away to the edge of a lake, with snow-capped peaks rising out of the mist beyond. All across the heath were slender indistinct forms that were at once trees or bushes, and at the same time *something else*. I saw her shiver a little as she went on, "Somehow they had become men, or animals, and as they looked out at me their faces were full of cunning and a dreadful malice. At that moment I felt quite terrified."

But needless to say Alexandra's curiosity overcame her fear, and she reached out to touch the picture. As she did so, M. Villemain suddenly cried out, "Be careful. You could be pulled in."

"Into what?" she asked in alarm.

"Into the landscape. It is dangerous."

By now I was quite caught up in this strange story. I leaned forward in excitement. "And what happened then?"

Alexandra shrugged. "That is all that happened. I felt all at once overcome with a terrible fatigue. And so we went downstairs for toast and tea."

I longed for more. It was as though Alexandra had strayed to the edge of faerie, and returned to tell me only half the tale.

She laughed, as though to dismiss it all as fancy, but there was an edge to her laughter that told me the experience had left her shaken. In truth, I am beginning to fear a little for Alexandra, in case her boldness and her curiosity may take her into places better left unexplored.

CHAPTER NINE

June 28

With the first volume of *The Secret Doctrine* so near to completion, HPB continues to work twelve hours a day, scarcely pausing to eat and refusing to rest between six in the morning and six in the afternoon. But her health is poor, and the Countess makes no secret of her concern. The doctor has confided that HPB's kidneys are in an alarming state, and her blood so full of enormous crystals it is only through a miracle she is still alive. As well, in spite of all her success, HPB's spirits seem very low. She so misses the family she left behind in Russia that she has written to her sister Madame Vera, asking her to come to London and live at Lansdowne Road. And so Madame Zhelihovsky is to arrive next month, with one of her daughters, who is also called Vera. The younger Vera is near my own age. The Countess says she is pretty and high-spirited, and will do much to enliven the household. However, we will be very crowded, and I wonder how much longer there will be a place for me here.

June 30

I must record what has just happened so perhaps I can make sense of it. Otherwise I know for certain it will disturb my dreams.

This evening HPB invited into her sanctum two society ladies who had come in hopes of seeing elemental spirits, vanishing tea-cups, astral letters, or any other curious phenomena HPB might produce. When the ladies had admired the photo of one of HPB's Tibetan Masters, the mysterious Mahâtmâ Morya, which sits in a place of honour on her desk, and when she had amused them with some card tricks and astonished them with astral bells, they asked her, rather slyly, to make the carved wooden tobacco box disappear. Cheerfully, HPB obliged. The box vanished, and though the ladies looked for it everywhere — even under the hem of HPB's robe — it was nowhere to be seen. Then, as mysteriously, it reappeared. The visitors, clearly delighted with this exhibition, thanked their hostess and took their leave.

This stage magician's performance struck me as unworthy of one so gifted, and so erudite. HPB must have read my thoughts, for she said, "Well, Miss Guthrie, why do you look at me so? I have given them what they came for, have I not?" And since she seemed to be inviting the question, I asked — as many others have asked before me — "Madame Blavatsky, is that real magic you do, or jiggery-pokery?"

HPB does not easily take offense, and this made her laugh. "Mostly the second. But never question, Miss Guthrie, that I can do the first. Shall I show you?"

When I hesitated, she turned those brilliant azure eyes upon me, and said, "Listen then, and learn. This is magic. This is the music of life. And have no doubt that it is real."

And from somewhere there came a ghostly music, faint and distant at first, so that I strained to hear; then growing louder till it filled that snug, close, lamplit room. It was high and sweet as the sound of a flute, but unlike any instrument I could name. With that intense and piercing sweetness came a scent of herbs — wild thyme, or rosemary — so that I thought of the Pipes of Pan, of their dangerous music, beckoning and enticing.

And now I could hear voices singing — a melody without words that made my heart catch in my throat. The voices, languorous and seductive, twined themselves around me. I could not move, could scarcely draw my breath. More than anything in the world I wanted to yield to that music, let it wash over me and transport me. My gaze drifted to the photo of the Tibetan Master. His eyes, dark and wise and beautiful, seemed to say, "Leave this world behind. I will lead you over the high lonely passes." And I was filled with a terrible foreboding. I remembered Alexandra's story of the painting, with its haunted landscape, and her words — or Villemain's: *"Be careful. You could be pulled in."*

But pulled into what? I knew only that I must step back from a nameless peril.

I felt flushed and feverish, and as tired as if I had not slept for days. When I turned to the darkening window, where the curtains were not yet drawn, I saw that HPB was slumped in her chair in a kind of trance state, oblivious to the world. On her face was a look of uttermost serenity; and I guessed that she was wandering, still, in some far place where I dared not follow.

CHAPTER TEN

July 5

On Sunday afternoon the two gentlemen from the Psychical Research Society, Mr. Barker and Mr. Grenville-Smith, are planning to visit a medium in Crouch End, to investigate her claims of spirit-raising. Alexandra, who is keen to accompany them, has invited me to join their party. But it seems that HPB takes a dim view of spiritualists. Our proposed adventure, which seemed to us innocent enough, inspired one of her impassioned dinner table lectures.

"I have been present at many of these séances," she informed us, "and they have filled me with horror and disgust. I have seen how a reanimated shadow will pretend to be someone's mother, or sister, or husband, or dead child, so that the person goes into perfect ecstasies, embracing this soulless, disembodied spirit, and imagining it has come to persuade them of eternal life."

HPB was looking straight down the table at me. I felt myself blush scarlet under her outraged glare.

"If only they saw, as I have often seen at these Spiritualistic séances, a monstrous bodiless creature seizing hold of someone. It wraps itself around its victim like a black shroud, and slowly disappears as if drawn into his body through his living pores."

What a hideous image those words evoked! The very thought of it made me shudder. When Alexandra called this afternoon for tea, I told her at once of HPB's warning. "We must make our excuses to Mr. Barker and Mr. Grenville-Smith," I said.

And what was Alexandra's response? *"Mais c'est incroyable!* Reanimated shadows! Disembodied spirits! I must see these for myself!" And though I pleaded with her to let me beg off, she would not hear of it. "You must come along to chaperone," she said.

This from Alexandra, who scoffs at our English sense of propriety; who goes on unescorted outings with M. Villemain and visits him alone in his room! But she was quite insistent, and so in the end, much against my better judgment, I have agreed.

July 8

Neither HPB's ominous words, nor my own apprehension, could have prepared me for what I now must write.

This afternoon, as we travelled in Mr. Barker's hired cab along the Bayswater Road, I had no inkling of what lay ahead. Mr. Barker had been quick to reassure us that a séance was no more frightening than a pantomime and its horrors no more real. "HPB," he told us, "suffers from an overwrought imagination, no doubt brought on by Turkish cigarettes." And so I was easy in my mind as we rumbled our way to Crouch End, thinking only of what curious place names are to be found on the map of London, which I have been studying of late. In Shepherd's Bush, surely, there are neither shepherds nor bushes; nor are there any elephants in Elephant and Castle. Tooting makes me smile; and then there are the places best avoided, like Shoreditch, Cheapside, Limehouse, Spitalfields, the Isle of Dogs. "Crouch End" made me think of some enormous hunkering animal. In my idle fancy I imagined it swallowing up the medium's house, walls, roofbeams, corner-posts and all.

Alexandra, meanwhile, wanted to know why Theosophists looked so unkindly upon spiritualists, when both were preoccupied with the world of spirits.

"Ah, but mademoiselle," said Mr. Barker, "you must understand that the shades called up by the Spiritualists are, as HPB would have it, mere imposters. They are nothing but shells, or empty envelopes, forever separated from their souls. In the hope of invading the bodies of the living, they pretend to be their departed friends and relatives."

"And Madame Blavatsky's spirits?"

"Those are another case entirely. HPB's spirits are not the common garden variety spooks conjured up in a séance. She would explain that they are lofty-minded apparitions, steeped in a superior brand of oriental wisdom, and meaning only good to humankind. They visit us in order to communicate arcane secrets — or simply to observe what is going on."

Alexandra took a notebook from her reticule and carefully wrote down his answer. Then she said, "I have been reading about the work of your Society. Do you mean to test this medium Mrs. Brown with electrical currents, galvanometers and the like?"

Mr. Barker laughed. "I'm sorry to disappoint you, mademoiselle. This is only a preliminary visit, to see if there are any grounds for further investigation. Chances are, this

Mrs. Brown will entertain us with the usual sorts of tricks that can only deceive a true believer."

"And what are those?"

"Oh, wires and draperies, dummy hands, phosphorous oil — any number of ingenious devices," said Mr. Grenville-Smith.

Alexandra turned to smile at him. Though he seems an amiable young man, as a rule he does not say much, and is perhaps a little shy in female company.(And Alexandra, goodness knows, can be intimidating.) Alexandra says he is the youngest son of a titled family, though I would never have guessed this from his unassuming manner. If I was in my old life still, we would never have met at all, still less be sharing a cab like friends and equals.

But what does any of this matter now? Before I try to sleep, I must describe, as plainly and as rationally as I can, the dreadful events of this afternoon.

There were of course no crouching beasts in the leafy streets of Crouch End. The medium, as it turned out, lived in a pleasant brick house, with potted geraniums on the step, and ivy clambering up the wall. The maid led us into a parlour which on that warm afternoon seemed as close and stuffy as HPB's own, though the smell was of beeswax and, more faintly, of boiled cabbage, not the incense and cigarette fog of Lansdowne Road. All the windows were closed and I thought perhaps Mrs. Brown, like HPB, was an old lady who suffered from the cold. But I saw when she came to greet us that she was no older than my mother, who is not yet forty. I had not considered how a medium, a caller up of spirits, might look — would she be draped in scarves and a-jangle with ear-baubles like a gypsy, or modishly Bohemian like Mrs. Morgan? I had surely not expected this small, plump, ordinary looking person in a severely buttoned, unpretentious black silk dress.

When we arrived, half a dozen people were chatting quietly amongst themselves. There were a pair of elderly ladies, alike enough to be sisters, dressed all in black; two younger, fashionably gowned ladies much like the ones who often called at Lansdowne Road; a middle-aged gentleman of military bearing, with a large moustache and a cane; and a pretty sad-faced young woman of twenty or so. And finally, there was a woman in a business-like coat and skirt who was introduced as Dr. Elliot. Her role, Mr. Barker explained, was to make a thorough search of Mrs. Brown's person, to be sure she was not concealing any devices or props.

The medium, Mrs. Brown, opened folding doors into another somewhat larger room. Unlike the outer parlour, which was cluttered with sofas and small tables and potted palms and china ornaments, this held only a large round oak table encircled by chairs, and a chest of drawers on which were displayed some musical instruments — an accordion, a guitar and a tambourine. At the far end of the room a curtain had been drawn aside to reveal a wooden cabinet about three feet wide, reaching from floor to ceiling, with front panels of some sheer fabric. When we had all gathered in this inner room, we were invited to find places at the table. Here too the curtains were close-drawn. On that bright summer afternoon we sat in a sweltering and oppressive gloom.

While we waited, Mrs. Brown disappeared into a side chamber with Dr. Elliot. When after a little time the two returned, Dr. Elliot gave an approving nod to our two Cambridge gentlemen, and the séance proceeded.

Now Mrs. Brown closed the curtain that concealed the cabinet (which had already been thoroughly searched by Mr. Barker and Mr. Grenville-Smith), and withdrew behind it.

"What happens now?" asked Alexandra, leaning over to whisper in Mr. Barker's ear.

He replied, in an ordinary voice, "I believe Mrs. Brown is entering her mediumistic trance."

"Perhaps we should sing," one of the old ladies in black suggested. "Oh yes, 'The Power of Love Enchanting'," said her friend. She led off, and everyone joined in.

"Now we are to clasp hands . . . " said the second old lady — the other chiming in " . . . and we should remove our gloves." Again we obliged.

For a while there was silence. I sat between Alexandra and one of the fashionable ladies, grasping their warm, sticky hands in mine.

Then, in that dim, uncertain light, we saw the tambourine rise of its own accord from where it rested on the chest of drawers, and float gently ceilingward as though wafted on a draught of air. At the same time the accordion gave forth a few desultory chords. From behind the curtain — and presumably from within the cabinet where Mrs. Brown sat entranced — there came a low, hoarse groan, and a kind of gurgle. Then unexpectedly a male voice said, "My dear, are you there?"

At once the first old lady replied, "My dear William, indeed I am here. Where are you? Are you speaking from the Other Side?"

"I am," said the voice. "And I have come to say that you need have no concerns about me, for this is a very pleasant place, and I am most happily situated."

At which news the old lady gave a cry of pure joy. And I thought to myself, *Well, that is easily enough done, Mrs. Brown need only be clever enough to disguise her voice, and she could be anyone's dead relative.*

But then there came instead the sweet, piping voice of a young child, asking "Is my mother there?" The sad-faced young woman gave a gasping cry and half-rose from her chair. "My baby, my baby!" she called out. But one of the elderly ladies put her hand on the mother's shoulder to restrain her, saying, quite sharply, "You must never enter the cabinet while the medium is in trance. To do so, could kill her." She added, more kindly, "You must not be distressed, my dear. Your child is happy and content in the spirit world."

But the poor young woman, still grasping the hands of her neighbours, strained forward across the table as though desperate to reach her dead child. And I thought, if this was deception, as surely it must be, it was a cruel trick indeed to play upon that anguished mother.

Then the curtain stirred as though a gust of air had caught it, and the candles flickered out. Hand in hand we all sat damply waiting. And then in that stifling dark there appeared an apparition, human in form, but with only the vaguest suggestion of a face, and bathed in a shimmering, otherworldly light. From head to foot it glowed like quicksilver, marshfire, ghostlight. Frail luminous threads trailed behind it; and all down one side, from shoulder to waist, was a vivid crimson slash.

The apparition spoke in a hollow, sepulchral voice — the voice, one imagined, of a soul that that was lost in the black void beyond the grave. "I have been most grievously wounded," it declared, and there was a world of sorrow and recrimination in those words. "In the bloom of my youth I was cut down, and died of my wound, and now my spirit knows no ease."

"My word," said Mr. Barker, "that's rather effective. I wonder how she does it?"

"There must be a secret compartment," whispered Mr. Grenville-Smith. One of the ladies of fashion gave him a stern look, and shushed him with a finger to her lips.

Then the military gentleman spoke. "Spirit, tell us your name."

"I have no name. I am a nameless spirit wandering in the void."

"An initial, then," the military gentleman persisted, as cheerfully as if this were a game of charades.

Once again that desolate, disembodied voice: "The letter is G."

Suddenly I could not breathe. My heart thudded against my ribs. A wave of nausea rose into my throat, and I felt darkness sweeping over me. I sensed that heavy oak table rocking on its legs like the flimsiest of washstands. Everything seemed to be shifting, tilting; I heard a rushing like a strong wind, (*how can that be*, I thought in my confusion, *when the windows are tight shut?*) the sound of glass or china smashing, a series of loud thumps, voices crying out in alarm. And then I must have fainted dead away.

I woke to find myself lying with my head in Alexandra's lap. Someone had undone the top buttons of my blouse, and Dr. Elliot was holding a vial of smelling salts to my nose.

The military gentleman was saying with apparent puzzlement to a now wide awake Mrs. Brown, "I cannot think why the young lady was so upset. As sure as I stand here, that was the ghost of my old comrade-in-arms Henry Gordon, dead these thirty-three years of a sabre wound at Balaclava."

But he was wrong. I knew the name of that awful spirit as surely as I knew my own.

It was George who had come to show me the fatal wound I had inflicted upon him; George who had come to accuse the murderess who had taken his life.

CHAPTER ELEVEN

July 9

The worst is not, so long as we can say, "this is the worst."
My father used to quote that, when everything in our lives
seemed to gang agley. It comes from *King Lear,* and it means,
I suppose, that as long as we still have our wits, and breath
to speak, we have not come to the worst place of all.

Yet how can I believe that worse is still to come? There
is no pretending now that George's wound was a small one,
quickly healed. For certain he is dead, and by my hand. And
am I any less a murderess, not remembering how I came to
strike the blow?

Nor do I remember much of yesterday, after waking
in confusion from my faint. I recollect Mrs. Brown, the
medium, looking pale and discomposed, I suppose because
of the disturbance I had caused, and perhaps also because
her china candlesticks were smashed. I remember the odd
way that Alexandra looked down at me, as I first came
round. And I remember the kindness and concern in Mr.
Grenville-Smith's eyes, as he gave me his arm and helped
me to a cab. But I deserve neither his good opinion nor his

friendship. I shrink from the thought that he might one day learn the truth.

July 15

I can scarcely bear to write of what happened yesterday, it gave me such a fright. After dinner HPB was vigorously holding forth on the Spirit World to the usual gathering of visitors, when she broke off with a kind of shudder in mid-sentence. Her next words so shocked me so that I nearly cried out. She said, *"A murderer has just passed below our window."*

A ripple of excitement ran round the room, and everyone turned to stare at HPB. Lady Asquith, who was sitting near the window, looked out at the street, but said she could see no one. My heart was thudding wildly as I waited for HPB to turn accusing eyes in my direction. This was a woman who could see what was invisible to others, who could peer into the darkest corners of my heart. Surely she must suspect that the murderer, far from being in the street outside, was under her very roof.

All last night I lay awake, listening to the clock strike the hours, fearful of what the morning might bring, and yet HPB has said nothing. Perhaps she is only biding her time, because for the moment I am useful to her. But she is not a patient woman, and she has no tolerance for mistakes. Suppose one day she should fly into a rage with me, as she does sometimes with Mr. Bertram? There are names she could call me far worse than the ones she calls poor Mr. Bert.

How foolish I was, to think I could find refuge in a city where no one knew me, nor cared what I once was.

July 21

Now that Madame Zhelihovsky and her daughter have arrived HPB seems in much better spirits, and I believe her health has also improved a little. It is hard to be downhearted in the younger Vera's presence. She is such a blithe and carefree young woman, quick to laugh, and every bit as pretty as the Countess described her. Needless to say she is much admired by the gentlemen of the household, and has especially caught the eye of one of HPB's protégés, Mr. Charlie Johnston. He has just graduated from Dublin University, and is to leave for Bengal in the autumn, but in the meantime is spending every possible moment at Lansdowne Road. Of course, this romance has greatly annoyed HPB, as she is much opposed to the whole institution of marriage.

At barely seventeen, it seems, she married General Blavatsky, a man three times her age. When at the altar the priest said, "Thou shalt honour and obey thy husband," HPB clenched her teeth and muttered, "Surely I shall *not.*" And promptly ran away to Central Asia.

All the same, I believe that Mr. Johnston and Miss Z. will marry. He is as handsome and clever as she is charming, and it is clear that they dote upon one another. But I felt a little melancholy this evening, as I watched the two of them stroll through the garden arm in arm. I remembered how, when I looked in Edith's mirror for the face of my future husband, there was naught to see but darkness.

Meanwhile, next month we are expecting a Colonel Olcott, who is coming from America to see HPB on some contentious matters of Theosophical business, which I will not attempt to explain. All these things seem to conspire against the timely completion of the book.

August 26

It's weeks since I have written in this journal. I think sometimes it would be better not to write at all, so there will be no record of this awful summer. The entire household is caught up in HPB's frantic efforts to prepare *The Secret Doctrine*. This vast work is soon to be published, and still she makes changes and additions, until we are all driven to distraction. Some of the corrections are HPB's own, but others appear on her desk as pages of foolscap covered with notes in blue pencil handwriting — the work, we are told, of the Tibetan Master Koot Hoomi, delivered by astral post office.

To make matters worse, HPB herself is unwell. She suffers from a great many ills, any one of which, says Mr. Archie, would kill an ordinary woman. In consequence she flies into tantrums for the most trivial of reasons.

Yesterday one of the foolscap sheets from Master Koot Hoomi was misplaced, and by afternoon, in spite of all our efforts, still had not been discovered. Just as we were sitting down to our tea, the two Messrs. Keightley, the Countess, Mr. Mead and myself, HPB came raging out of her study to demand why we had given up the search. "Here you all are, lazing about, doing nothing, and without this information it is quite impossible for me to continue!"

Mr. Archie said mildly, "We will continue to look, HPB, as soon as we have had our tea. Surely the paper cannot have vanished quite as mysteriously as it appeared."

This seemed to enrage HPB still further, and now, to my dismay, she turned her fury upon me. "You, Miss Guthrie! Why do you sit there like a flapdoodle? Do you imagine you are being paid to gossip and eat toast?" I must have turned bright red in my embarrassment and confusion. Though she constantly berates poor Mr. Bert, HPB had never before spoken to me in this manner, and I was speechless with mortification. Though I half-rose to my feet, thinking to leave the table and continue the search, HPB would not be mollified.

"Here am I, day and night bent over my desk, wearing holes in the elbows of my sleeves, surrounded by flapdoodles, and as for you, Miss Guthrie, you are the most useless of all." And then she called me some names I would blush to write in this book. Even the steward, in my days as a bondager, had not so belittled and abused me. My throat felt tight, my eyes prickled. And then anger overcame humiliation. This woman I had so much admired now seemed to me a selfish, foul-tempered, ungrateful old harridan. Murderess I might be; but like everyone in the household, I had missed meals, lost sleep, laboured to exhaustion for her sake. I felt quite dizzy and sick with indignation.

HPB had worked herself into frenzy. She would not leave off shouting at me. All at once the teacups began to rattle in their saucers, and the milk jug, of its own accord, jiggled about on its tray and overturned. The open jam pot flew off the table, dragging the tablecloth after it, and almost landed in Mr. Archie's lap.

In the sudden silence we looked at one another in dismay. HPB, meanwhile, was staring at me as though it were I and not herself who had drenched the tablecloth and splotched the India rug with strawberry jam. Next time, I thought, she may aim the jam pot straight at my head.

Now it seemed sure that I would be turned out of the house to fend for myself. And at that moment I did not much care.

CHAPTER TWELVE

September 30

Looking back over my last entry, I realize how distraught I must have been to write those melodramatic lines. But here I am still at Lansdowne Road, and little has changed, except for the ever-increasing pace of work. Nothing more has been said of the incident of the flying jam pot which caused me so much distress, nor have any more murderers passed beneath the window.

I have not seen Alexandra for some time. She has written to say that she is occupied with her Oriental studies — though it is clear that she is also spending a good deal of time in the unsettling company of M. Villemain. Dear Alexandra! She is so worldly, and so eager to embrace every kind of experience. And yet sometimes I feel older than she, and much less innocent. When she shares her secrets I can only listen and offer none in return; for surely even Alexandra would shrink away in horror should I confess what I have done.

In her letter she relates another curious adventure with M. Villemain into what she calls the Unknown, the

Inconnu. She writes in French, for she is not as fluent in English on the page as she is in speech. It is a long letter, but with the help of a dictionary from HPB's study I have been translating it, a little at a time, as an exercise, and now I will transcribe it into this journal.

☾ ☾ ☾

"My dear Jeanne," (Alexandra writes)

"M. Villemain has been shut up in his room for several weeks, engaged in mysterious occult practices. Now that he has emerged, he looks so wraithlike that we are all concerned for his health. I decided he might benefit from a little fresh air and exercise. Also, I am anxious to learn more from him about this business of the peculiar painting that can entrap the onlooker. And so I asked him if he would like to come with me to visit the Crystal Palace outside London, where there are concerts and dramatic entertainments. Somewhat to my surprise, he agreed. We made plans to leave early and spend the whole day.

"But I had forgotten how quickly these autumn fogs descend. I woke to find the city shrouded in mist. By the time we were ready to leave the fog had not lifted. '*Quel dommage*,' said M. Villemain, and proposed that we wait for a better day. However, I had set my mind on this expedition. 'This is England,' I pointed out. 'There may not be a better day.' At the station we could scarcely make out the shapes of the carriages. 'Surely the afternoon will be fine,' I said by way of encouragement. And so we boarded the phantom train, and set out through a veiled and mysterious landscape.

"M. Villemain — who can be a very dull companion — seemed lost in his own thoughts."

(Ah, so the intriguing M. Villemain has turned out to be not quite so *intéressant* after all!) But to continue the story:

"There was nothing to be seen through the windows, and lulled by the swaying of the carriage, I must have drifted off. I woke suddenly as the whistle sounded and the train came to a sudden stop. Looking out, I saw that the fog had lifted. But where were we?"

When Alexandra asked a man on the platform, "Is this the Crystal Palace station?" he gave her a very strange look and shouted to the conductor, who told them to get off the train as fast as they could. "How you will smile, Jeanne, when I tell you that this sophisticated traveller had fallen fast asleep on an express train bound for Edinburgh!"

The train whistled and went on its way. Alexandra and M. Villemain were left standing alone on the platform in an autumn drizzle, with no idea where they were, waiting for an evening train that would take them back to London. The ticket office was closed, and the countryside was deserted.

"Not a tea shop nor even a farmhouse to be seen. And it had begun to rain harder, and so we huddled in glum silence on a bench under the porch roof. I was cold, and hungry, and feeling both foolish and thoroughly annoyed. 'Well, here is an adventure,' I said to M. Villemain. To which he responded in a mournful tone, 'Perhaps we are dead.'

"I stared at him. 'Dead? Whatever are you talking about?'

"'We could be dead and not even know it. Why would an express train stop for no apparent reason and set us down in this desolate place?'

"Surely he was not serious! I said that there must have been an obstacle on the track.

He replied, in a voice heavy with foreboding, 'It happened in exactly that way to a member of our Gnostic Society.'"

And then M. Villemain told Alexandra this extraordinary tale. It seems that a man was on a holiday trip with his wife and young son when their train inexplicably stopped. They could hear and see nothing: all the outside world was hidden by a thick white fog. To the man's surprise his wife took the child's hand and began to lead him from the carriage. Not sure what to do, the man followed his wife, who seemed to know exactly where she was going. When they came to a hedge, the mother and child somehow found their way to the other side; but the man could not follow, for his way was barred by a tangle of thorny branches. As he sought desperately for a way through, he heard a voice calling out, "You are not expected." Beyond the hedge he could see, growing ever more distant, the vague shapes of his wife and son, but it was impossible to reach them. A great weariness overcame him, and as he drifted out of consciousness he heard a far-off voice repeating, "You are not expected."

When he awoke he was in a hospital. It seemed that he and his family had been in a terrible train crash. The mother and child had passed into another world, where they were expected. In spite of his serious injuries the husband would recover, and so he could not break through that thorny hedge into the world beyond.

Alexandra said, in a joking way, "Well, you and I, M. Villemain, I believe we are not yet expected." But she was astonished to realize that he was in deadly earnest.

"All this is most intriguing,"she writes, "and I mean to study further the various theories about the afterworld, and the spirits of the dead. In meantime, however, since we would be so late getting back to London, I proposed to buy M. Villemain a good dinner in a restaurant, for there would be no hope of getting anything to eat at the Supreme Gnosis."

In any event, Villemain now seemed in a mood to speak of occult matters, so Alexandra seized the opportunity to question him about the strange incident of the painting.

Why, she wondered, was he afraid that she would be drawn into his painted landscape?

And in reply he began another story, as strange as the first.

A woman — like Villemain an initiate into the occult arts — was viewing a painting of an African landscape, an oasis with palm trees.

As she looked into the painting, she became lightheaded, and it seemed to her that she had somehow entered the painting and was walking among the palm trees, under the hot equatorial sun. For a while she wandered about in the desert, wiping her face with her handkerchief. Suddenly the light changed, she felt a violent shock, and she found herself in the artist's studio, where it seemed she had fainted. She went to take out her handkerchief, but could not find it. Then she looked at the painting. There was the missing handkerchief, clearly painted into the picture, at the foot of a palm tree where she had dropped it. .

"Ever since," Alexandra continues, "I have been puzzling about the explanation. Was it merely a collective hallucination? Villemain himself, and others who have seen the painting, swear that previously, no handkerchief had appeared in the scene; but from then on it was clearly visible. It makes me think, Jeanne, that there is much we have not yet discovered about our world.

"Villemain has offered a theory, and I will try to explain as best I can. He says that every landscape in the real world, and even a painted landscape, has its counterpart on the astral plane. So, for example, if an artist paints a picture of a meadow or heath, he has not only created a design on canvas, he has also created a heath or a meadow on that other plane of existence. And herein, said Villemain, the danger lies: each of us also has an astral counterpart, a kind of insubstantial twin. If we are not careful, that astral form could be seized and held captive by this other world that exists on the edge of our own.

"Needless to say, all this makes me wish to explore the subject further. And so, although we did not see the Crystal Palace, the day was not a total loss; and before we took a cab back to our lodgings, we found an excellent Italian restaurant and I bought M. Villemain the fine dinner I had promised."

CHAPTER THIRTEEN

October 7

T hough the Messrs. Keightley feared the book would never see completion, at last the preface is written, and the first volume of *The Secret Doctrine* has gone to press, with Volume II, *Anthropogenesis,* to follow in December. At Saturday's At Home there was a great air of celebration, and also of relief.

Miss Vera and Mr. Johnston are to be married, with HPB's grudging approval. Once she gave up grumbling and calling them flapdoodles, she offered to make arrangements for the wedding at the Russian Church, and even plans to attend the ceremony.

However, their romance has caused an uproar in Theosophical circles. It seems that when Mr. Charlie Johnston first joined the Society he saw it as a sort of holy vocation, swearing never to marry, and encouraging all the male Theosophists to do the same. Mr. Willie Yeats finds this very amusing, and he teases Mr. Johnston at every opportunity. . One night when Miss Vera was not present,

Mr. Yeats remarked, "And to think, Charlie — were it not for love, you could have become a Mahatma!"

Meanwhile, Mr. Yeats has got together a committee to perform experiments based on Theosophical writings. Somewhere he read that if you burned a flower to ashes, and then set the ashes out in the moonlight for several nights, the ghost of the flower would appear. Since coming to Lansdowne Road I have learned that many improbable things may be possible. Still, I do not think this experiment will succeed.

He has also got hold of some indigo powder which supposedly has special properties, and has asked the members of his committee to put it under their pillows, and record their dreams. I am relieved that he has not asked me to do this. I would not wish to relive the dreams that sometimes come to me in restless sleep: stones falling from the air; footsteps echoing behind me on an empty street; an endless railway journey, rushing into fog and night; and too often, the apparition of George's wounded and accusing ghost.

We had not seen the two gentlemen from the Psychical Research Society for some time, but on Saturday they joined us for an early tea. As they were about to take their leave, Mr. Grenville-Smith surprised me by saying, "You are quite pale, Miss Guthrie. HPB has kept you slaving far too long over that manuscript. You look in desperate need of fresh air." And then — still greater surprise — he invited me on a Sunday afternoon excursion to Hampstead Heath, to see the autumn colours.

Truth to tell, I was quite flustered, scarcely knowing how to reply — would it be thought improper, in London, to set out unchaperoned? But the Countess gave me an encouraging smile, saying "What a splendid idea! It will put the roses back in your cheeks." And so, yesterday being fine and clear, we went by omnibus, and spent the whole of the afternoon walking on the Heath.

Though not as fashionable as Hyde Park, the Heath seems very popular on a Sunday with courting couples. Everywhere we saw young women in beribboned bonnets, walking out with their young men on their afternoons off. Wandering across the autumnal meadows and along the woodland paths carpeted with golden leaves, I could almost imagine myself in the Borders once again; and I was happier than I have been for many weeks. Though all the same it disturbed me to see men offering rides on poor starved looking donkeys — these Londoners seem to care very little for the treatment of their animals — and I said so to Mr. Grenville-Smith.

I was not sure why Mr. Grenville-Smith had invited me, but I could not imagine it was merely for the pleasure of my company, for I have so little conversation to offer, and he is accustomed to the clever talk of Cambridge folk, and it seems is a landed gentleman besides. But come to that he does not talk a great deal in any case, seeming content enough to stroll by my side in the misty October light. Once though, he turned to me with a smile, saying, "Your hair, Miss Guthrie . . . " and I put up an anxious hand to my head, wondering if my sailor hat was askew, or my plaits, as they often did, had come unfastened. But then he pointed to a maple along the path ahead, bright with autumn reddish-gold. "Look," he said, "the leaves are exactly the colour of your hair!"

For a while we watched the kite-flyers, and the children sailing their toy boats on the boating pond. And then we climbed to the top of Parliament Hill, and saw all of London spread out before us.

I must confess that I took great pleasure in *his* company, friendly and undemanding as it was. I guessed that it was my place to make conversation, and so I asked, "Are you also a professor of zoology, like Dr. Barker?"

He laughed. "Someday, perhaps. With a great deal of luck. At present I'm merely a research fellow — a much less evolved species. But I work with Dr. Barker, and it was he who interested me in the Society for Psychical Research."

"And what is it exactly that the Society researches?"

"Well, in the main, four areas: astral appearances, transportation of physical substances by occult means, precipitation of letters, and occult sounds and voices. So as you see, your Madame Blavatsky is a veritable motherlode of research material, since she claims to practise all four."

"And is she a fraud, as Dr. Barker says?"

"Ah, Miss Guthrie, on that question the jury is still out. I respect Professor Barker's opinion as a scholar and a scientist. On the other hand, it's always best to keep an open mind. This is why we continue to gather evidence."

And that of course was no answer at all, but I could see I would have to be content with it.

"But what of you, Miss Guthrie? Do you have plans for the future? Do you mean to stay on at Lansdowne Road?"

"As long as Madame Blavatsky has work for me. But once this enormous book of hers is published, I may no longer be needed."

"And then?"

And then? It is a question I often ask myself, when Madame B. grows so impatient that she threatens to cast us all out into the street; or when she is so ill, and so in despair, that we cannot believe she will ever complete the work.

"Perhaps . . . " What could I tell him? "Perhaps I will find some work in a bookshop, or with a publisher . . . "

"And would you enjoy that sort of work?"

"I think I might." And then, because he was gazing at me so attentively, with such friendly interest, I grew bolder. "Once a long time ago I imagined I would like to write my own books, to be an author."

I feared he might laugh at that foolish notion, but instead, he said, "Only once a long time ago? Miss Guthrie, I hope you have not given up that ambition."

That threw me into confusion. "I don't know . . . one day, possibly. But I don't mean the kind that Madame Blavatsky writes. I think I would like to write books . . . "

"That people actually want to read?" he finished for me. And I had to laugh, because that was precisely the thought in my mind.

"We are two of a kind then, Miss Guthrie. I'm making my own attempt at authorship — I hope one day to publish my investigations into psychic phenomena. And I warn you, my views on your employer may not be entirely flattering."

"No more are mine," I replied. "Especially when she calls me a flapdoodle." And it was his turn to laugh.

If my steps had slowed a little, it was because I did not want the afternoon to end. But after a bit he said, "We have walked quite a long way. Are you tired? Should we stop for tea?"

I shook my head. "I like to walk. At home in the Borders it was the only means of getting about."

"Though I hope you're not in the habit of walking alone, Miss Guthrie. London is not the Borders. It's a dangerous city — especially now."

"You mean the killings in Whitechapel? But surely he only attacks women . . . "

"Of a certain reputation?"

I nodded. And then fell into an embarrassed silence. As bondagers, with only women present, we might have spoken of such things freely. But this was London. One did things differently here; and this was a highly improper conversation with a gentleman I hardly knew. But if Mr. Grenville-Smith noticed that I was blushing, he chose to overlook it.

"I doubt, these days, that any woman is entirely safe on any street." He gave me a very grave, intent look. "You *will* promise me, won't you?" And of course I did, and was surprised and flattered by his concern, though there is not much likelihood of my ever walking alone through Whitechapel.

So far I have written very little in this journal about Mr. Grenville-Smith. What shall I say, now that I am alone, with no one to see my blushes? He is quite tall and rather spare of figure, though he does not slouch and lounge about in the London fashion that some young men affect, but carries himself in an upright, straightforward way. Rambling along in his tweedy jacket and soft cap he seems like someone more at home in the woods and fields than in a Mayfair salon. What else? He is fair-haired, and his eyes are a smoky shade of grey. He has a strong chin, which my mother always said was a sign of character in a man; and he smiles not only with his mouth, as some people do, but with his eyes as well.

But how foolish of me to think such things, let alone to write them down. I, with my fingers still calloused from the stitching of turnip-sacks; with my rough Borders speech that still clings to my tongue, hard though I try to talk as Londoners do. A cat may look at a king, they say; but how can a bondager think to look at the son of a lord? Even supposing that she were not a murderess.

Nonetheless, I retired last night in quite a giddy state of mind, and was scarce able to sleep. But the cold light of Monday morning brings with it sober reflection, and I have now reminded myself why Mr. Grenville-Smith comes to Lansdowne Road. It is not to enjoy the society of our fashionable guests, and not to admire HPB, but rather to investigate her. And surely that must have been the real purpose of our outing? "We continue to gather evidence," Mr. Grenville-Smith said. If he should befriend me, and gain my confidence, what secrets might I reveal — what new evidence for the Psychical Research Society?

CHAPTER FOURTEEN

October 13

I n the Borders, the harvest will be in, and the turnips waiting to be lifted. There will be frost in the early mornings, mist trailing through the woods and over the shorn fields, the smell of woodsmoke. And then by midmorning the sun will burn away the haze and flood the hills with golden October light. But here in London, autumn is the season of sulphurous fogs that shroud the shops and houses, turn the streets into dim smoky tunnels, and creep with sooty fingers over every threshold.

At Lansdowne Road the gaslights burn all afternoon so that we can see to work; and outside, the street is filled with swirling yellow mist. Though we are busy every day with last minute work on *The Secret Doctrine*, HPB still keeps to her habit of Saturday At Homes, and yesterday Alexandra paid her first visit in weeks. When she rose to leave the Countess suggested she should take a cab, for the afternoon would soon be drawing in. "With these terrible murders at Whitechapel," she said, "it is not safe for any young woman to walk the streets alone."

Alexandra, quite unworried, assured the Countess that she would venture nowhere near Whitechapel; but having spent her allowance on books and a new winter bonnet, she must pinch pennies by taking the train as far as Gower Street. And so I offered to walk with her the short distance to Notting Hill Gate station.

The fog had thickened, muffling sound and hiding the tops of the houses and trees. As the yellowish-grey gloom grew deeper, I said to Alexandra, "Surely it would be wiser for you to stay for dinner, and spend the night at Lansdowne Road." But she laughed and shook her head.

"From all accounts, HPB's astral entities are so active at night they are likely to disturb my sleep. I have heard too many tales of mysterious midnight rappings, and lamps that turn off and on without reason and icy Himalayan air blowing into people's bedrooms. I believe I will take my chances with the fog."

Since Alexandra seemed unafraid, I made up my mind not to show my own anxiety, though the two of us were quite alone on the deserted street. I told myself that it was not yet mid-afternoon, and I chattered some nonsense or other to keep my spirits up. But how often the thing we fear most lies in wait until our attention is distracted! Just before we reached the station, there stepped from out of the fog a tall, cadaverous figure that blocked our way with outspread arms so that we could not easily pass.

I had a quick, terrified impression of sunken eyes in a gaunt unshaven face, lank hair escaping from under a dark cap, a long flapping coat of some indeterminate shade. And in one hand, the glint of a knife blade.

I could think of nothing but those terrible stories of the Whitechapel fiend. My throat clenched, my knees threatened to give way. I clutched Alexandra's shoulder, unable to speak or catch my breath.

"Give me your money," this apparition said. And Alexandra, who must have been no less terrified, answered in a steady voice, "I have only my train fare. Take that if you wish." And she reached into the pocket of her coat. I could see her hand trembling as she held out a shilling piece.

He took the coin with a kind of grunt, and then turned to me. "I have no money with me," I managed to say. It was the truth.

"Rings? Pocket-watch?"

Dumb with fear, I could only shake my head. And I watched in silent horror as he raised the knife.

I cannot say what happened next. I have no clear memory of it, only that something shifted within me, my terror turning to a mindless and unmindful rage. The air all at once was filled with flying pebbles, pieces of brick and broken cobblestones, as though some giant hand had scooped them up and flung them in blind fury at our attacker. I heard him cry out in pain, saw him throw up his arms to cover his head, then sink to his knees as bricks and stones and cobbles plummeted mercilessly down upon him. And then Alexandra seized me by the arm and we fled headlong back down the street to Lansdowne Road.

❰ ❰ ❰

Needless to say, there was no question of Alexandra's leaving Lansdowne Road before morning; and today I have sand behind my lids and a head full of cotton wool, for we talked far into the night. After such an experience I should have been wide awake, my mind in a turmoil and all my nerves on edge. Instead I felt strangely lethargic, and as the night wore on, the bizarre events of the afternoon began to blur.

"I believe I'm sickening for something," I complained sleepily to Alexandra. "All my bones ache."

"Small wonder," she said, a little tartly. And then to my surprise she reached out and took my hand. "Jeanne," she said, "can it be possible — don't you realize what you did?"

In my heart, I must have known what her next words would be. "Jeanne, there is this power in you . . . "

No, I thought. *No*. And I turned away my head like a child who stubbornly refuses to hear.

"Listen to me, Jeanne, *chérie*. Remember the séance. It was not the medium who made the table rock, or the candlesticks to fly into the air. It was not she who unlatched the window and made a great gust of wind sweep through the room."

"But those are the tricks a medium uses to fool her audience. Mr. Barker explained it all."

Alexandra made no reply. In that awkward silence she seemed to be waiting for me to speak.

Finally she said "Do you not understand? *Vraiment?* Jeanne, the medium was as astonished as any of us who were in that room. You were so dreadfully upset. You went as white as if you had truly seen a ghost, and there was a strange distant look in your eyes, like someone walking in her sleep. And then the table began to rock, and the candlesticks smashed, and after a minute you gave a terrible cry and fell down in a faint."

And because I was angry with HPB, the tea things flew off the table . . . and because I was frightened of George . . .

And then I was weeping inconsolably on Alexandra's shoulder. I had guessed the truth these many months — and dared not let myself believe.

CHAPTER FIFTEEN

October 20

T oday Volume I of *The Secret Doctrine* arrived from
the printers. Such excitement, to see at long last the
fruit of our labours! For HPB I know it was a moment of
pure happiness in the midst of the darkness that has come
to surround her.

She tells us that she is "old, rotten, sick, and worn-
out" — and in truth, her appearance is shocking. Jaundice
has turned her skin almost the colour of coffee, and her
legs are so painfully swollen that it is only with the greatest
difficulty she can move about. Dr. Mennell has prescribed
a daily dose of strychnia for her kidneys, though I cannot
see that it is doing much good.

Still, in that ruined face her eyes still blaze with the same
intensity, and by sheer determination she continues to work
at the same exhausting pace. There is her magazine, *Lucifer*,
to edit, as well as helping with a new publication, *La Revue
Theosophique.* Then too she has begun work on a third
volume of *The Secret Doctrine*, about the great occultists.
All this as well as preparing forty or fifty pages of instruc-

tions each month for her students, doing research for the meetings of the Blavatsky Lodge, and composing a manual to explain Theosophy. And because none of these things bring in money, she must also write articles for her Russian newspapers.

Worried about HPB's failing health, the Countess laments, "You've taken on far too much! You are doing the work of half a dozen people."

To which HPB replies, "How fortunate then, that I can be in two or three places at once!" She tells of a journey through the Caucasus Mountains when she became too weak and ill to travel by horseback, and so was sent by riverboat to stay with friends in Tiflis. As the boat cut its way between two steep banks, her servants were astonished to see their mistress gliding out of the boat and across the water towards the shore — while at the same time her body still lay unconscious in the bottom of the boat. "There have been times," she says, "when I was in another far-off country, a totally different person from myself, and had no connection at all with my ordinary life."

With HPB one can never be sure if such stories are true. Still, I am reminded of M. Villemain's strange tale of the woman who wandered into a painted landscape, while her other self lay asleep in a chair.

Today also Mr. Charlie Johnston and his new bride Vera sailed for India. After the liveliness of the summer, the house seems very quiet and empty. What lie ahead for me, I suppose, are long dull winter days filled with interminable small tasks.

October 22.

With this morning's post, a letter from Alexandra. She has made up her mind to leave London in the New Year.

CHAPTER SIXTEEN

November 11

I am writing this at the big table in the dining room, amidst a clutter of books and papers and tea-things. Rain is clattering on the roof; fog hides the drenched ruins of the garden. The curtains are drawn against the early dark.

There is little for me to do today. On this dismal late afternoon HPB has given up the struggle to write and instead has taken to her bed.

She is very ill. The Countess emerged from her bedroom just now, looking wan and tired. I know that she was sitting up with HPB for most of the night. Still, says the Countess with a pretence of cheerfulness, HPB has been nearer to death than this several times before, and astonished her doctors by a full recovery before the day was out.

Lately the weather has discouraged visitors, but on Saturday, when the sun broke through for an hour or two, some ladies from Bloomsbury came by to be entertained by mysterious knocks and rappings, vanishing objects and astral bells. In our audience as well was a tall, thin, sharp-featured woman dressed all in black, who, sitting well apart from the West End ladies in their feathered hats, kept a keen eye on the proceedings.

But HPB was clearly not herself.

"I fear that my astral energies are at low ebb today," she told them. I expected that she was about to beg off the usual occult demonstrations. (In fact, I was paying very little attention, for I was thinking how very alone I would be when Alexandra went home to Brussels; and also wondering when Mr. Grenville-Smith might pay another visit.)

All at once I became uncomfortably aware of HPB's eyes upon me. There was an odd expression on that ravaged face — the look, I thought, of someone struck by sudden inspiration. "Miss Guthrie," said HPB. "Be kind enough to lend me your assistance. If you will come over here and take my hand . . . "

I rose at once and went to stand beside her chair. She reached up and seized my hand in hers. "What I require, Miss Guthrie, is to tap into your astral energy, and add it to my own."

She must have seen my look of alarm, for she added, quite kindly, "Don't be distressed, there is no risk to yourself. You are young and strong, you have energy and to spare, while mine is fast weakening; and it will not do to disappoint these ladies."

I cannot describe exactly what happened after that. There was a sensation of warmth in our joined hands, and I could feel a pulse throbbing painfully behind my eyes — though that may only have been my nervousness and apprehension. I was shivering, and at the same time my face felt hot and flushed. That was all. But suddenly there were knockings and bangings all over room: beneath the table, in the cupboard, above the ceiling, behind the walls. These were not the genteel rappings of astral spirits with drawing room manners; but loud, disturbing noises like objects falling from a height, or hammer-blows.

Afterwards, the ladies were agreeably mystified, a little frightened, and undeniably impressed. I stole a glance at HPB. She looked wrung-out, exhausted; but as usual after these sessions, entirely pleased with herself.

As for myself, I took no pleasure at all in that curious performance. I felt dull and listless, wanting only to sleep. I fear that from now on I may have a new role to play at 17 Lansdowne Road — one that I would never willingly have sought.

November 12

Today another note from Alexandra, who has something *"très important"* to tell me. I have arranged to meet her this Sunday for a walk in Kensington Gardens, if the weather prove not too inclement.

November 18

How splendid to escape for a few hours from Lansdowne Road! This morning a cold wind blew up and swept away the worst of the fog, so that the day, though chilly and damp, was clear enough for our expedition. The Countess loaned me a warm waterproof cloak with a hood, and as I set off on the short walk to Kensington Gardens, I was in quite good spirits. Alexandra was waiting for me by the Round Pond. The park was almost deserted today, being too late in the year for the children with their toy boats, and too early for skating. Alexandra wished to see the Gardens' collection of rare shrubs and trees, hoping to find some from the oriental lands she planned one day to visit. As we strolled along the wooded paths, now slick with fallen leaves, I reminded her of her message.

"You said you had something important to tell me? More important than to say you are abandoning me to live in Brussels?"

Alexandra looked up from examining a botanical label. *"C'est vrai*! Much more important! I have been to the Reading Room of the Museum, for I wished to learn about this peculiar talent of yours." She looked at me in that earnest way she has, when some new pursuit has stirred her interest. "I thought to find it only in the occult section. Of course we know what Madame Blavatsky believes — that such things are the work of elementals. And others say they are caused by the restless spirits of the dead, or by demonic forces. But *quelle surprise*! — there are also scientific papers written upon it. I found learned articles, by serious men of science — physicists and physiologists who have been conducting experiments. They call it psychokinesis, and they believe it may have to do with a superabundance of psychic energy."

How my father would have approved of Alexandra! She is the scholar that he dearly hoped I would become. The more obscure the fact, the more arcane the topic, the greater delight she takes in hunting it down. But I was only half attending to Alexandra's explanation. I was remembering instead a story from the Borders.

When Alexandra paused for breath I told her, "There was a kitchen maid in Galashiels who made all the crockery fall down and smash. When she was in the room, mustard pots and flat-irons hurled themselves at visitors, and washing hung to dry on hedges flung itself into the road. Everyone said she was possessed by the devil, and wanted to have her exorcised, or possibly drowned."

"But you, *ma chère* Jeanne, I do not believe you are a demon, or a ghost, or an elemental spirit. You have a talent — a wild talent, *certainement* — but I do not think there is anything diabolical about it."

So, I thought, perhaps I am not an instrument of Satan after all — merely a sport of nature. There was little enough comfort in that.

"Jeanne, why so *désolé*? This is a marvellous gift you have."

A gift, I thought bitterly. *What value is a gift that in one heedless moment of anger can make a murderess of you?* But I could not speak of that to Alexandra. Instead, I told her of my fear that I must now assist HPB with her entertainments.

"And is that so very terrible? Perhaps she will increase your wages."

How could she speak so lightly of my predicament? For Alexandra, this fearful talent was a curiosity to be studied; for me, it was a burden weighing down my soul.

"But how am I to control this power? It only comes to me when I am angry, or afraid."

Alexandra laughed. "Living at Lansdowne Road, I would not find that so very difficult." But then I think she saw how upset I had become, for she added more seriously, "Surely you are controlling it when Madame Blavatsky joins her energies with yours?"

"It seems so," I admitted. "But her energies are quickly failing."

"To me," replied Alexandra, "the answer is clear. One refines whatever talents one may possess, by determined practice. Listen, *chère Jeanne*. I have been reading about the sorcerers of Tibet." (What a lot of Alexandra's sentences begin with, "I have been reading about . . . "!) The ones who are called *lung-gom-pas* have mastered strange powers through special training. It is said that they can cross in a few days a distance that should require a month of travel; or by special breathing make their bodies light enough to float. And some, it is said, can even project their thoughts. All this is accomplished, I believe, through mental concentration."

"But why would I wish to levitate, or let others hear my private thoughts?"

"Don't be a goose," said Alexandra. "That is quite beside the point. I am saying that you must learn to master your own gift, so that it is under your command."

"But how shall I do that? And if you please, Alexandra, no more talk of Tibetan sorcerers!"

"As I have explained. Through mental concentration. You must promise to begin practising, this very night."

And so I promised, though I find the prospect disturbing, and I have little idea how to begin.

We had planned to cross the Serpentine into Hyde Park to watch the ladies of fashion promenading, and the gentlemen riding their thoroughbred steeds along Rotten Row; but now the wind had dropped and a dank yellow fog was settling in. Wiser, we decided, to seek the warmth and safety of our lodging places; and so we embraced and parted.

Now, while I have an hour before bed, I must put down my pen and practise this peculiar art of mental concentration.

November 19

We are shut in by fog so thick and black that it is like darkness fallen at midday. It presses against the windowpanes, a smothering mud-coloured wall. HPB has taken to her bed; the rest of us, heavy of spirit, move about in a perpetual gloom. Since I have no tasks with which to occupy myself, I will write of what took place last night.

"A superabundance of psychic energy," Alexandra had said. An energy that arrives unbidden, with the power to maim and to kill. But also an energy that can serve me, and serve Madame Blavatsky, if only I can learn to summon it at my command.

How to begin? I set the inkpot in the middle of my writing table and stared at it, rapt with contemplation. Concentrate as I might, it remained steadfastly in its place.

Fear. Anger. Those were the keys that could unlock the power. But who would wish to relive the worst moments of her life?

Nevertheless.

Memories came to me: of how HPB had so unjustly berated me; of how a man who might so easily have been the Whitechapel killer stepped out that night from the fog. I thought of George's sly, hateful grin as he tormented me. I recalled with shame and horror the sight of his spilled blood, and his terrible, accusing ghost. My heart began to race, my teeth chattered, my jaw clenched with remembered dread.

Pens rattled in their jar. Loose papers flew about as though scattered by a gust of wind. The inkpot skittered like a mouse across the polished surface and teetered on the table-edge. I snatched it up an instant before it toppled to the floor.

November 24

Word has spread across London, it seems, of last fortnight's psychical performance, and so yesterday we had a great crowd of ladies come to call, including Lady Margot Asquith and two of her friends. There was also a gentleman from one of the London papers. As well, Dr. Conan Doyle, the author, had come up from Portsmouth. When by chance I found him standing at my elbow I gathered up the courage to address him: saying how much I had admired his "Study in Scarlet" that I had read in Beeton's Christmas Annual.

How often I had imagined this, when I was a foolish lass still under my father's roof: the ladies in their crêpe de chine and velvet, the learned gentlemen, the clever talk of plays and books. I had seen myself as the centre of such a gathering — a woman of letters, celebrated in my own right. But I am no less a hireling here, than in the Borders. No one, seeing me hovering at HPB's side in my plain skirt and shirtwaist, would imagine me anything but a servant. Still, Dr. Conan Doyle was cordial enough, and promised to send me a copy of his next detective story.

But Madame Blavatsky was not, as they imagined, restored to health and vigour. In fact she has been so ill that she was barely able to rise from her bed. And so, with the greatest reluctance, I agreed to help with the proceedings. Everyone gathered in the dining room to await the celebrated thumpings and bangings and chiming of invisible bells. But this time, there was no warmth, no sensation of shared energy when I reached for HPB's hand. Clammy and lifeless, it lay inertly in my clasp: the hand of a woman sick unto death.

It is hard to recall what thoughts went through my mind at that moment. HPB had been kind to me, after her fashion, had taken me into her household, and for that I was forever in her debt. I did not wish to see her humiliated before her admirers, or belittled in the press. My God-fearing Scottish parents had taught me to be honest, always, for to practise deceit is to do the Devil's work. Yet how much deception had I already practised, since the day that I murdered George?

And so, in her name, I did what HPB was no longer capable of doing. What had been unconscious and unwished for, now became a purposeful act. This time I found it easier. My thoughts reached down to that painful knot of memory, and as quickly glanced away.

It was enough.

Unseen objects clattered and thudded in cupboards. Bells rang. The gaslights flared, dimmed, and flared again. Sheets of paper fluttered through the air. A bookshelf leaned out and flung its contents to the floor.

The newspaper gentleman scribbled urgent notes. From the London ladies, there were gasps of astonishment and delight; from HPB, pale and exhausted in her chair, an enigmatic smile; and from the Countess Constance, hovering in the doorway, a glance that told me she understood more than she was likely to reveal.

CHAPTER SEVENTEEN

December 15

The twenty-fifth of December is fast approaching. The date meant little to me in the Borders, for bondagers worked that day as on any other. But the fragrance of spices in the kitchen has reminded me that in London Christmas is a season of festivity. And tonight I am quite foolish with excitement over a promised Christmas treat.

Mr. Grenville-Smith came round this afternoon, to say that he had been given tickets to *The Yeomen of the Guard*, and would be glad of company. The Countess did not feel she could leave HPB for the whole of an evening (it being quite out of the question for HPB herself to attend) and neither of the Keightleys it seems are fond of operetta. But Mr. Mead, though he always seems so solemn, confessed a great affection for the works of Messrs. Gilbert and Sullivan.

"Splendid," said Mr. Grenville-Smith. "And Miss Guthrie? You'll join our party?" This invitation, offered so offhandedly (perhaps a little too carefully offhanded?) took me by surprise, and I could not think what to answer.

"Ah," he said, colouring a little, "but of course you must have another lady to keep you company. Since the Countess has declined, perhaps Mlle David . . . "

"Yes, of course," said I, all flustered and thinking what a gowk I must seem. "I will send to ask her."

And so on Wednesday we are to go by carriage to the Savoy Theatre. Needless to say I have nothing suitable to wear and Alexandra's skirts are too short for me, but the Countess, who is slender and about my height, has very kindly found me a plain skirt in bronze coloured silk, with a lacy bodice. I think it will do very well.

December 20

Last night I felt for a few hours like the heroine of a novel. Alexandra, arriving early by cab, did my hair in loops tied up with a ribbon, and made frizzy curls round my face. *"Voila!"* she said. "No more the *jeune fille*, now you are a woman of the world." And truth to tell, I scarce recognized myself.

"How elegant you both look!" declared Mr. Grenville-Smith when he came to collect us. That made me blush, though I'm sure the compliment was directed to Alexandra, who looked thoroughly Parisienne in her pearl grey satin. When one is strong and tall as I am, elegance is a forlorn hope. The very most one can wish for, I suppose, is to be considered handsome. As for Mr. Grenville-Smith, he looked quite splendid in his silk top hat and swallow-tail coat; though I believe I like him just as well in his soft cap and country tweeds. When our carriage pulled up to the entrance off the Thames Embankment, he took my arm and Mr. Mead took Alexandra's, and so I felt like a lady of fashion in my silk and lace.

The Savoy is quite a modern theatre, and the very first to be lit by electricity, and so we stepped out of the dark and fog into a great dazzle of light. The interior is very grand — all plush seats and gilt and rose-red walls, marble columns and hundreds of glowing incandescent lamps. Our seats were in the first row of the balcony, so we could look down and admire the gentlemen in their evening dress and the West End ladies in their low-cut bodices all aglitter with beads and sequins. Presently the lights dimmed, the rustle of programmes and chocolate wrappers stilled and the orchestra struck up.

Mr. Grenville-Smith had brought opera glasses so that we could see close up what was happening on the stage. The songs were clever and the voices seemed to me enchanting (though Alexandra, who has trained as a singer, was more critical than I). But the story was not so comic as I had expected.

When Wilfred, the Assistant Tormentor, made his vulgar advances on poor Phoebe the Sergeant's daughter I could feel my stomach knotting and a flush spreading over my cheeks.

I knew if I dwelt on bad memories, untoward things might happen — lamps begin to sway, lights flicker; so I stayed as calm as I could, and thought instead of the play, and the sad plight of the dashing Colonel Fairfax, unjustly condemned to death . When he sang so plaintively, "Death, when e'er he come, must come too soon" I had to take out my handkerchief, and Mr. Grenville-Smith gave me a quizzical look .

Before long the plot grew so complex, with so many mistaken identities, that I was quite lost attempting to follow the twists and turns, hoping only that in the end

Phoebe would marry Colonel Fairfax, whom she loved. But it was not to be so. When the curtain fell, everyone seemed to be married to the wrong person, which in novels seldom happens, though I think often enough in real life. I thought how fortunate that Miss Zhelihovsky and Mr. Charlie Johnston had found each other, if even in an operetta things could go so badly awry.

December 21

Now that both volumes of *The Secret Doctrine* have been published, HPB has become even more famous, and several gentlemen from the newspapers have come to interview her. HPB is pleased with the articles, and the journalists all seem very impressed with HPB. Of course we have saved the clippings.

Mr. Willie Wilde — brother of the famous Oscar — writes for the Telegraph, and is a regular visitor to Lansdowne Road. He does his best to make sure that nothing written in his paper is unflattering to HPB. But other journalists seem equally susceptible to her charms. The gentleman from *Picadilly* (November 2, 1888) writes, "A Russian by birth, and of good family, Madame Blavatsky was as a child endowed with extraordinary powers of clairvoyance, and following the guidance of her intuition, she gave her whole energy to the study and development of her higher faculties, and to the source of those mysteries and occult powers which underlie the secret wisdom religion of the ancients." And he says he cannot do justice to the "eloquent words that fall from the lips of this gifted woman."

And here is the article in *The London Star* (December 18) which says that Madame Blavatsky "reveals herself as a lady of exceptional charm of manner, wonderful variety of information, and powers of conversation which recall the giant talkers of a bygone literary age."

This is the side of HPB that visitors see, and the Theosophists who every Thursday evening sit at her feet in silent adoration. We who live with her every day are aware that she can also be rude, and stubborn, and selfish, and infuriating. No one knows this better than the Countess Constance, who has dedicated her life to HPB's service. I think that even the Countess came close to losing her temper, on the day that HPB was to have her photograph taken in Regent Street. Because the day of the appointment was wet and windy, HPB refused to leave the house, announcing that the bad weather would surely cause her death. "See, I do not even own a cloak," she said, "because I never set foot outside. Besides, who would want a picture of this loathsome, ruined old face?" The Countess, who can be just as stubborn, went round the house borrowing furs and shawls and scarves, and found a sort of Russian turban with a veil to tie over HPB's head. Still Madame B. refused to stir from her chair — no matter that the cab had been sitting outside for hours.

"I cannot go," she declared. "You must want me to die. You know I cannot step on the wet stones."

"Enough," said the Countess. "Jeannie, ask the cab to wait a little longer." She told us to fetch some carpets and lay them from the front door all the way to the carriage. When gusts of wind lifted up the carpets, the faithful Countess — who had once been the wife of the Swedish Ambassador — held them down with her own hands.

HPB's friend Mr. Edmund Russell, who had suggested the photograph, went along in the cab, and later told us the rest of the story. "Disembarkation was even worse! I had to coax her into the studio, saying 'Come along, Your Majesty' — and once up the stairs, she flatly refused to sit for the photo."

But Mr. Russell made her laugh, and in the end, she agreed. We all thought the photograph turned out well, HPB looking wise and dignified and serene, with one hand propping up her double chins.

CHAPTER EIGHTEEN

December 22

T his morning the weather was much improved, and I
went with the Countess to Oxford Street to purchase
Christmas cards. As we stepped into the bookshop I heard
a familiar voice in conversation with the bookseller. My
heart began to thump in a disconcerting fashion; and when
I glanced into the natural history section there was Mr.
Grenville-Smith taking down a large book from the shelf.

"Miss Guthrie!" he exclaimed, looking round. "What a
pleasure to see you again!" And truly he did look happy to
see me.

"Mr. Grenville-Smith! Will you be spending Christmas
in London, then?" And as soon as the words were uttered I
wished to have swallowed them, they sounded so coy and
forward. How I envy Alexandra her Parisian aplomb and
her gift of conversation.

"Alas, no, I'm off home to Wiltshire on the morning
train." Catching sight of Countess Wachmeister, he greeted
her with a cheerful wave. "My compliments, Countess."
Then turning back to me he said, "I hope you were not too

disappointed in *The Yeomen of the Guard*. It seemed to me a little dark, and perhaps not their best effort."

"Oh, but it was wonderful," I exclaimed — for I could not bear to think he imagined me disappointed.

"I only wish you could have seen *The Mikado,*" he said. "That was a splendid production. I hope one day there'll be a revival."

Meanwhile he had set his book down on a table, and I stole a glance at the title. It said, in French, *New or rare animals, collected during an expedition in the central parts of South America.* He gave me a rueful smile. "In eleven volumes, and beyond my means at present. One rarely finds an unbroken set — I come here from time to time to admire it." He lifted the book and opened it, almost reverently, I thought, to hand-coloured plates of exotic birds and reptiles. He unfolded a map to show me routes marked out in various coloured inks; and then turned to some tinted drawings of tropical landscapes.

"They're very beautiful," I said. "And what place is that, Mr. Grenville-Smith?" At least I think that is what I said — we were standing very close and truth to tell I scarce remember, though I ken well enough what he replied.

"It's Brazil," he told me. "A country that one day I hope to see for myself. But 'Mr. Grenville-Smith' — how elderly that sounds. I feel when I am called that I should be wearing a long beard and carrying a walking stick. My friends call me Tom, and we are friends, are we not, Jean Guthrie?"

And then he smiled down at me, and held my gaze, and I knew it was not just the look of a friend, but something far more than that. I cannot describe the pure happiness of that moment — a happiness that surely I do not deserve.

Though there was much I wished to say, all I could manage to do was to nod, and return his smile.

But soon after that we said our goodbyes, for it was growing late, and the Countess was fretting a little that Saturday visitors would arrive with no one there to receive them.

Before we left I bought a lace-trimmed card with cherubs for my mother, and one with a basket of kittens for the bairns, and I have put them into the post along with as many pound notes as I have been able to save.

As we drove home, I was happier than I have been in a very long time. When we came to Lansdowne Road there were carolers singing along the street, and I wanted to put my head out of the window of the cab and raise my voice along with theirs, in joyful celebration.

And then this evening a messenger came to the door and delivered a package with my name on it. I opened it to find a small grey paper-bound book of songs from *The Mikado*, and a card that was signed simply "Tom".

December 26

We have had a quiet Christmas, much confined to the house, with Madame Blavatsky still unwell and the weather most days dank and murky. Also the papers were full of another horrible East End murder just five days before Christmas, so that even in Lansdowne Road we feared to venture out after dark to so much as post a letter. We had not bothered with a tree or decorations, but for tea on Christmas Eve we had iced fruitcake, and Mr. Archibald bought a bag of chestnuts to roast over the fire. There was of course no goose or turkey for Christmas dinner, but instead a special curried vegetable dish, with wine and plenty of plum pudding. The post brought a

Christmas card from Alexandra, all silk-fringed and gilded and embossed, that was greatly admired. But she is about to leave for Brussels, which seems a long way off, and I know that when she is gone I will feel very much bereft.

December 31

Tonight, in these last hours of the old year, I have been thinking of New Year's Eves at home in the Borders, when I was a child and my father still alive. I remember how the Hogmanay fires burned the old year out, how the midnight bells rang, and how we waited for a dark-haired man to step over our threshold, bearing gifts of coal and salt, black buns and shortbread.

I wonder what they do to welcome the New Year in that great house (as I imagine it) in Wiltshire. Are there bonfires on the downs, and bells pealing out? Perhaps Tom Grenville-Smith is alone tonight, as I am, sitting beside the fire with a book on his knee while he dreams about Brazil. But no, most likely there will be a ball, and it will be waltz music that he hears; and he will dance with ladies in low-cut Paris gowns in a blaze of lamplight, under glittering chandeliers.

These winter nights when I am abed with the candle blown out and I am drifting towards sleep, I find myself thinking how it would be to leave this cold grey city and live once again among woods and fields: not in a ploughman's cottage as I once did, but in a grand house with servants and many rooms, and one room entirely to myself, with shelves for my books and a desk upon which to write. And sometimes as sleep overtakes me, though I know it is daft to do so, I think of the one person with whom I would wish to share that house — or any house, be it only a ploughman's cottage after all.

CHAPTER NINETEEN

M*a chère* Jeanne,
C'est impossible. I can no longer remain in dreary Brussels, *en famille.* And so I have made new plans.

Have I spoken to you of my father's friend Elisée Reclus? He is a famous old radical who fought on the barricades for the Paris Commune. He and his circle are great believers in education for women. They have encouraged me to pursue the interests closest to my heart. Instead of resuming my studies in music, I intend to enroll in the *College de France* and study Sanskrit under the Tibetan scholar Professor Foucaux. Mrs. Morgan has arranged for me to lodge at the Paris headquarters of the Theosophist Society, and I will write again upon my arrival.

Numéro 30 boulevard Saint-Michel

Chère Jeanne,
So here I am in Paris, in the Latin Quarter, at the lodgings arranged for me by Mrs. Morgan. The Paris

headquarters of the Theosophist Society occupies the third floor above a grocery shop. I think I must inform Mrs. Morgan that she has been deceived as to the nature of the accommodation. In comparison, my lodgings at the Supreme Gnosis seem the very height of luxury. There are no other members of the Society in residence at the moment, and I believe I understand the reason.

My room, which opens directly off the dining room, is sparsely furnished and quite shabby. There is no bathtub in the house, merely pitchers and a washbasin on a table in my room. Mme Jourdan, my landlady, has advised me to use the bath establishment down the street. Dinner last night was boiling water, in which there floated a few lonely fragments of potato and a soggy chunk of bread.

When I first arrived, I did not know whether to laugh or to weep. But then I told myself that this is an adventure, and I have never turned away from an adventure. And in any case, Jeanne, you know that I never cry.

Now I must go shopping, for the house is not well heated, and no one has offered me extra bedding. And after that I must look for another place to stay.

Alexandra

CHAPTER TWENTY

Twelfth Night, 1889

T he holly wreath has been taken down from the door; the Christmas cards tied up in ribbon and tucked away in drawers. At home in the Borders, in the long dark days that lie ahead, I would have much to occupy my time: grain sacks to mend, dung to spread on the cold fields, straw to bunch up to make shelters for the lambing. Here, though the Countess finds small tasks for me, I have too much leisure for thinking of the past, and dwelling on the uncertainties that lie ahead.

The year has not begun well for Madame Blavatsky. The Theosophists are in a state of disarray, with HPB in London, and Colonel Olcott in America, battling each other for control. HPB has expelled from the Society both the president of the Blavatsky Lodge and one of the lady members, Miss Mabel Collins, on the grounds that they were flirting For good measure, she has expelled an American lady for gossiping about it. Now Miss Collins is suing HPB for libel. HPB seems to quite enjoy banishing people — Mr. Willie Yeats says she is like a cat let loose in a cage of canaries.

All the same, her health is continuing to fail. She works as hard as ever, sitting at a little table in her study, scribbling occult symbols in chalk on the green baize cover; but she tells us she feels like a poor sick donkey dragging a cart of rocks uphill. "Not only am I betrayed by this rotten, worn-out body," she announced the other morning, "but by the cruel slander of my friends."

Much as *The Secret Doctrine* has been praised in Theosophist circles, the critics have not been kind. The Keightleys, who have been keeping watch for reviews, are becoming quite discouraged. *The New York Times* has called the book unreadable and incomprehensible, and *Science* magazine has called it a great contribution to comic literature. Distinguished orientalists have attacked her scholarship, and the editor of the *Religio-Philosophical Review*, from whom HPB expected better, talks about her "extravagant absurdities".

Worse yet, it seems that the Himalayan masters have abandoned her. The tinkling of astral bells, and the rapping on tables that she calls the psychic telegraph, have fallen silent. Lamp flames no longer flare up of their own accord after they have been put out. A wind cold as a gust from the Himalayan peaks no longer blows through HPB's overheated rooms, nor does the inexplicable odour of incense. The broken cuckoo clock in her study no longer greets visitors with peculiar sighs and groans, and no written messages from the Mahatma appear on her cluttered desk.

"The Masters are angry with me," HPB tells us sadly. "I must have made some error that offended them."

Our most frequent visitor is Dr. Mennell, looking sombre as he increases her strychnia prescriptions.

And now, at this worst possible time, Dr. Oliver Lodge is coming to Lansdowne Road to investigate HPB's ability to perform miracles. Dr. Lodge, who like Tom is a member of the Psychical Research Society, is interested in all manner of psychic occurrences. He is also a distinguished physicist, an expert in the study of electrical currents. It is a pity he did not choose to visit when Madame Blavatsky was in better health, for a good report could do much to restore her reputation. What a rebuke to her enemies, if a respected Doctor of Science can be persuaded of her powers! But suppose he, like so many others, decides that she is a fraud?

Countess Constance seems more than usually tired and distracted. "We must do whatever we can to help our dear Madame Helena through this trying time," she told me with an anxious smile; and I understood well enough her unspoken message.

CHAPTER TWENTY-ONE

February 14

T hough I know that Mr. Grenville Smith — (no,) Tom — is once again busy with his work at the university, still I have found myself listening for the doorknocker every weekend on the chance that he might have returned to London. I even thought of finding some pretext to visit the bookshop on Oxford Street, in the faint and foolish hope of finding him there.

Now, in this dreariest part of midwinter, with a sickroom atmosphere descended upon the house and little work to do, I have found my spirits very low. But then today a note was hand-delivered to our door.

My dear Miss Jean Guthrie, you have languished far too long in Madame Blavatsky's haunted drawing-room. I fear I may discover you all wan and pale and listless as a Gothic heroine. Be that as it may, I am in London till Sunday evening, and planning a visit to the Zoological Gardens. I would be most pleased to have your company. May I call round to fetch you, Sunday at ten?

Tom

How quickly a few words can lift one from the depths of melancholy to the heights of joy!

February 17

Tom came this morning by cab to fetch me, and we set out through streets that as usual were muffled in fog. Then, as we came to Regent Park and the entrance to the Zoological Gardens, a pale winter sun broke through, and the shapes of trees and buildings gradually revealed themselves. "A fine morning after all," said Tom, as he signed the members' book at the gate. "What splendid luck!"

And so with the day before us, we strolled along the Broad Walk, stopping first to admire the lions. On Sundays the gardens are only open to members of the Zoological Society, and so, said Tom, there was not the usual throng of spectators crowding around the lion house, jostling for a better view. After that came the sea lions' pond, and then the conservatory where the monkeys live. Tom told me all the names of the various sorts of monkeys, and the countries from which they came. As I watched them at their lively play, like so many naughty children, I could see why Professor Darwin says they are the ancestors of us all. (That seems more likely than HPB's idea that we are evolved from super-beings who once inhabited the lost continents of Lemuria and Atlantis.)

Then we went through a tunnel into another part of the Gardens, to see the elephants and rhinoceroses, the hippopotami and giraffes. Exciting though it was, to observe them close at hand, it made me sad to think how these great beasts, who once had roamed the wide plains of Africa, must be confined in a London park. When I said this to Tom, he nodded, and I guessed that he felt much the same.

"If all goes well," he told me, "I hope soon enough to observe them in their natural surroundings."

"In Africa?"

"Indeed, in Africa, and what an adventure that will be! But you, Jeannie, have you thought that one day you would like to travel?"

No one else, not even the much-travelled HPB, had ever asked me such a question. But Tom seemed to be inquiring out of genuine interest. My first instinct was to say, "I've found my way from Scotland to London, and that was quite adventure enough!" But then I remembered my pleasure and excitement when I first discovered the travel journals in my father's library. What romantic visions were conjured up, as I read of Arabia Felix, and the Mountains of the Moon, and Petra, the Rose-Red City half as old as time. That was when I was very young, not yet suspecting what the future held, so that all things seemed possible. "Sometimes," I told Tom. "But only in daydreams. I can't imagine such a thing could ever come about."

"One never knows for certain what may lie ahead." Tom offered me his arm as we went down some steps, and I had the foolish thought — quickly put out of mind — that to passers by we might seem like a courting couple. Tom said, "If your mind is made up, if you want something badly enough . . . I was meant to go into the army, or the clergy, or heaven help me, law. And instead I chose zoology." He added, with a grin, "My father was not well pleased."

I had once imagined all scholars to be pale and thin and stooped from biding too much indoors. But Tom is not yet a professor, and he seems more at home in the woods and fields where his research takes him, than in a stuffy lecture hall. And when I stole a sidelong glance and saw the sun glinting all gold in his yellow hair, though I tried hard to think about the birds and beasts in their cages, it was lines from the Song of Solomon that rose to mind. They were words I had loved when I was but a young lass still at home, and full of dreams. *His mouth is most sweet; yea, he is altogether lovely. This is my beloved, and this is my friend, O daughters of Jerusalem.*

And if that makes me shameless, well, we cannot help our private thoughts.

❰ ❰ ❰

Presently, when Tom looked at his pocket watch, we saw that it was well past luncheon, and so we decided instead on an early tea in the refreshment room.

"What a pleasant day this had been," I said, when we had settled ourselves at a table and given our order. "It was most kind of you to invite me."

"The pleasure is all mine. And I felt it my duty to rescue a fair maiden from the dragon's lair."

I laughed. "Madame Blavatsky is not really a dragon," I said, "though at first I thought her so. She has been kind enough to me in her own way. Truth to tell, she is just a very sick old woman. And who would not be bad-tempered, plagued by ill health, and exhausted by overwork?"

"And tormented by her critics. It cannot be pleasant to be called a fraud, a forger and an imposter."

"But the members of your Psychical Research Society — do they agree she is a fraud?"

"She may well be. Certainly Richard Hodgson was convinced of it. All these miracles she performs — the astral bells, the letters appearing out of nowhere, the magically vanishing and re-appearing objects — all those can be managed by secret compartments, by clever accomplices, by simple sleight of hand."

"And yet . . . "

He set down his teacup, waiting for me to continue. But what was it that I wished to say? That when you lived day in and day out at Lansdowne Road, you saw and heard things that could not easily be explained? Or that I had discovered powers in myself as inexplicable as any of HPB's?

I found I could not finish the thought. I asked, instead, "And you, Tom? What do you believe?"

He was silent for a moment, as though considering his reply. Then he said, "A scientist is meant to keep an open mind. There is so much in this world that we have yet to discover. I would like very much to believe that Madame Blavatsky's talents are real. I understand that Dr. Lodge is planning to do his own investigation. If he is convinced of her authenticity, think what possibilities, what new areas of research that would open up! But if indeed she is a fraud, then she is no better than any of the so-called psychics and mediums who have set up shop all over London to delude the innocent, by taking advantage of their naiveté and their grief. And those I consider ordinary criminals, who deserve to answer before a magistrate for their misdeeds."

At those words my mouth went suddenly dry, so that I could scarcely swallow my mouthful of watercress sandwich. I am not a fraud — I know I am not — but nonetheless if I have murdered George then in the eyes of all the world I am a criminal. How terrible, in the midst of such happiness, to be reminded that one day I may have to answer for my crime. These past weeks, with some time to reflect, I have told myself that perhaps George was not dead after all, but only injured, and it was my guilt that made me see his vengeful ghost in the medium's parlour. But, nonetheless, his wound was real enough — I saw the blood and heard his shouts of pain, — so I am still a criminal, though perhaps I might not hang.

Tom is kind and sweet-natured, and does not seem to mind a jot that I am not a beauty, and unfashionably dressed, and humbly born. But he would mind a great deal if he knew that the girl who sat before him eating scones and drinking China tea was an ordinary criminal, who one day must answer for her misdeeds.

CHAPTER TWENTY-TWO

Alexandra writes at length from 30 boulevard Saint-Michel:

"As you will have surmised from my last letter, life with the Paris Theosophists leaves much to be desired. I have already described their awful food (fortunately there is a cheap restaurant just down the street) and their scholarship is little better. They pretend to read the *Bhagavad-Gita* by comparing the Sanskrit word for word with a French translation, with no regard for grammar. And then they sit around for hours on hard chairs, meditating — until (so I'm told) their spirits leave their bodies and rise towards higher planes of existence. When my landlord M. Jourdan claps his hands and says '*Rentrez*', the disembodied spirits must return to their fleshly envelopes, which by now I think are getting very stiff and cold. One can only hope that all the spirits find their way back to their proper owners!"

Apparently the Theosophists of Paris believe themselves descended from ancestral beings who once inhabited the moon. "As you can imagine, it is hard not to laugh," writes Alexandra, "but they are very serious in their beliefs and I must try not to give offense."

I suspect that the Bohemian life is losing its charm for Alexandra. She adds that the Theosophists like to set out at midnight and wander through the streets of Paris until three or four in the morning. Then, "sustained by many cups of *café noir,* they talk until dawn." Alexandra is studying Sanskrit at the Collège de France with a Tibetan scholar, Professor Foucaux (though I expect all those sleepless nights are making it difficult for her to concentrate). Listening to him, she says, she has become more than ever determined to visit the Forbidden Kingdom. "So few Europeans have ever travelled there, not even the Professor himself." (Madame Blavatsky's Himalayan travels, we are both convinced, are a figment of her imagination!)

Alexandra goes on to tell how she has discovered the Musée Guimet, where she has been reading about the literature and philosophy of India and China. "There I believe I will find more mystery, more secret wisdom, than the inhabitants of the Boulevard Saint-Michel have ever dreamed of."

And she writes with great enthusiasm of a new acquaintance she met at the museum: "The Countess de Bréant — a most brilliant and intriguing woman, a student of Jewish and Arab philosophies, of Pantheism, and also of the Vedantas. She has travelled in India, and was interested to learn that I too hoped one day to visit the Buddha's birthplace."

Quite out of the blue this Countess invited Alexandra first for a cup of tea, and then to a meeting of the Pythagorean Society, of which she is a member. "As you can imagine, I was astonished and excited to learn that here in Paris there are devotees of the great Greek mathematician, who is almost a mythological figure, a veritable god of science. Of course I accepted her invitation."

And thus Alexandra embarks on another adventure. Much to her disappointment, I suspect, she could only attend the meeting, which was open to the public, but not the ritual ceremony at which only initiates were allowed. "And of course if there was a Society, there must be initiates! Everywhere, it seems, are these crowds of devotees and disciples, dedicated to the arcane mysteries of Egypt and ancient Greece.

"The Pythagoreans meet in a pavilion at the end of a little Parisian garden. The meeting room is large and austere, but comfortably furnished — very different from the cramped and wretched atmosphere of the Boulevard Saint-Michel. We seated ourselves on velvet-upholstered benches. Below the speaker's platform was an inscription, *Même si elle est trop haute*, which means that one should strive always towards one's loftiest ideals, even when they seem impossible to attain.

"Such an idea has always appealed to me. It is the journey that counts, after all — the adventure of the road, the excitement of the ever-changing landscape, the perilous ascent to the high peaks, with no certainty of what lies behind the mists. Perhaps, I thought, among the Pythagoreans I could learn to experience that sense of awe that has so far eluded me — the *terreur sacrée* that overwhelms our reason and can take us to the very edge of the unknown.

"Alas, *chère Jeanne, quel désappointement!*"

The assistants, she tells me, distributed the text of a very long *récitation* printed on expensive paper. Slowly, gravely and interminably, the members intoned the words. Far from being inspired with sacred terror, she found herself drifting off to sleep.

"Then the speaker referred to the formula written on one of the walls, and based on the writings of Pythagoras: *Le nombre est l'essence de choses* — 'number is the ultimate reality'. I hoped he would discuss this enigma further, but no — instead he began to explain how human souls are formed from the ether which fills space, and how after the death of the body, our souls go to live on various other planets, according to how much merit we have earned in life. It seemed to me this had little to do with mathematics.

"I thanked Madame Bréant politely for her invitation and excused myself, pleading the demands of my other studies. Still, I am not discouraged. I shall continue my explorations, wherever they may lead me."

CHAPTER TWENTY-THREE

February 18

U ntil now HPB has paid little attention to my comings and goings, so long as I was on hand when needed. However, my afternoon's outing to the Zoological Gardens did not go unnoticed, and as I passed by her desk on my return she fixed me with that riveting blue gaze. "About this young man from the Spookical Society — I have made myself entirely clear, I believe, on the subject of marriage."

This was so disconcerting that I scarcely knew how to reply. "Madame Blavatsky, if you mean Mr. Grenville-Smith, surely you must realize he is just a friend. There's no danger of anything more between us."

"So you say. But I know when someone is in danger of becoming a flapdoodle."

I wished to put an end to this absurd conversation. "If Mr. Grenville-Smith marries at all," I said, "it will be to someone of his own station."

"His own station," she repeated, with a hint of mockery. "And what do you imagine that station is?"

"He is the son of a lord, I believe."

"The youngest son of a baronet, to be precise," said HPB, and I knew from her tone that she intended to have the last word. Or in fact a great number of last words. "Since he won't inherit, he'll be expected to make his own way in the world, and since he has chosen to mess about in science, he'll be hard put to rub two shillings together. If he has any sense, he'll see that a healthy young wife with a good head on her shoulders will be more use to him than some anemic debutante." She stubbed out her cigarette with considerable force, by way of emphasis. "Marriage for a woman is a fatal step, Miss Guthrie. She is tied hand and foot to a master whom she is required by law to honour and obey. One should run from marriage as from mortal danger."

And that of course was what HPB herself had done. But I remember how Miss Vera's cheeks had glowed with happiness when she married Mr. Johnston; clearly, she saw her wedding as the beginning of joy and not the end of it. But sadly, I am not Miss Vera, whose beauty draws every eye, and makes men want to cherish and protect her.

Exactly as though she had read my thoughts (and most of the time, I believe, she does!) HPB said, "You sell yourself short, Jean Guthrie. You may not be a raving beauty, but you have those splendid green eyes — though you would not think it now, men have worshipped me for my eyes. You have an enviable shape, a graceful carriage, and a fine head of hair, if you would only look after it better. A good brain also counts for something. Tom Grenville-Smith is smitten, mark my words. You must take great care not to become entangled."

If only it were true! How willingly would I become entangled! But Tom I think sees me as a sort of younger sister, someone with whom to share his love of books, and theatre, and country rambles. It's only in novels that the sons of baronets fall in love with parlour-maids, or, less likely still, with the girl who hoes the turnips.

February 23

Professor Lodge has arrived, along with two of his colleagues from the Psychical Research Society. I caught a glimpse of them as I retreated from the dining room to HPB's study, where I am to remain till I am needed. I may be here for some time, so I have brought my journal with me, by way of keeping occupied.

I am feeling very anxious, thinking what I must do, and knowing how much the outcome of this day depends on me.

Madame Blavatsky has gone out to greet her visitors. Even with the Countess's help she could scarcely lift her great bulk from her chair. She seems immeasurably weary. Her eyes, once so piercing a blue, are dulled with pain.

As for Professor Lodge, he is a gentleman of middle years, with a full dark beard going a little grizzled, and a high gleaming forehead. He has a rather stern, intimidating look, and even Countess Constance, I think, is a little frightened of him. At the moment he is taking tea and talking to some journalists. From where I sit I can hear their conversation. Just now one of the journalists was asking the Professor, "How is that a man of science like you is interested in spiritism?" And the professor answered, rather sharply, "You mean in psychic phenomena? Is that any stranger than that I should be interested in x-rays? Not so very many years ago, those too would have been considered occult claptrap."

It is customary to have the subject of the investigation thoroughly searched, to be sure she has no apparatus concealed about her person. I remember that is what was done at the séance in Crouch End. But of course in the case of Madame Blavatsky, such indignity was out of the question. Just now I heard Professor Lodge conferring with the Countess, saying that without safeguards, the experiment would be flawed; followed by the Countess's whispered protestations, and then HPB's indignant roar: "Sir, do you imagine I am some humbug medium, conjuring up spectres in the dark? I, who am an impenetrable mystery of nature, an enigma for future generations? What need have I, for wires and devices?" And then there was a series of thumps, and I guessed that she was banging her walking stick on the floor for emphasis. Old and tired and sick she may be, with her powers failing, but her fierce pride is undiminished. It saddens me, to think that her reputation should depend on yet another sort of trickery.

But now I gather that they have found a compromise: HPB is to be seated well out of reach of any table, wall or cupboard that might conceal a mechanism; to which arrangement she has grudgingly agreed.

I hope that Professor Lodge does not expect one of HPB's celebrated miracles — like the chair made so heavy that three men cannot lift it, or the closed piano made to play as though by invisible hands. I cannot stretch and elongate my body so that I can touch the ceiling, nor can I produce the ghostly image of a Mahatma, emerging like fog from my head and shoulders. Unlike HPB, I cannot make solid objects vanish, still less make half a dozen appear where there was one before.

But I can make an entertainment of my own devising that I think will bemuse and astonish our distinguished visitor.

Now I can hear the tea-things being cleared away. It is time for me to play my part in this charade.

March 10

A fortnight has passed since I last wrote in this journal — a fortnight spent in shame and vain regrets. Yet had I foreknowledge, would I have acted differently?

I have determined to make this an honest record, not leaving out the things that are difficult to write. And so I must set down the disastrous outcome of Professor Lodge's visit.

Before our visitors arrived, the Countess asked Mr. Archibald to set up a tall japanned screen at the end of the dining room, just in front of HPB's study door. There I was to stand well out of sight, while HPB occupied her usual place in full view of our audience. I could see that the Countess was as anxious as I was myself. As I went to conceal myself behind the screen, she put a hand on my arm and said, with an apologetic smile, "Dear Jeannie, you do know that we would not ask this of you, if Madame were herself, and her powers not so weakened?"

I nodded, wondering as I did so, what hope there could be of Madame ever recovering her powers. How much more often was today's performance to be repeated, until that indomitable spirit finally succumbed?

I could hear HPB talking at some length about the Mahatmas, and how their invisible presences might manifest themselves. She was speaking, I thought, directly to Professor Lodge. Then came an expectant silence. I took a deep breath and focussed my thoughts. Countess Constance had placed a large vase filled with hothouse roses in the centre of the dining room table. Though I could not see the faces of my audience, I heard their delighted gasps as an invisible hand snatched up the blossoms and tossed them high into the air. There were appreciative murmurs, and a scattering of applause. I imagined Professor Lodge sitting astonished with a lapful of crimson roses, stray petals caught in his beard; while HPB acknowledged the applause with a faint smile and an imperious nod of her several chins.

Some extra chairs were ranged against the far wall, and now I set them teetering and hopping in a demented two-step. The trick with the roses had been easy enough, but now, with this greater effort, I felt the first hint of dizziness and nausea that I knew would soon grow more intense. But who could deny, when they saw those madly dancing chairs, that this was psychic energy, and not mere sleight of hand?

What I planned next I knew would leave me weak and gasping, but that was a small price to pay, I thought, for proof of HPB's powers. I focussed my mind upon the dining room table, heard it creak and groan in all its joints. I might have been lifting a mountain on my shoulders, as I strained against its inert weight. My head began to ache as though a chain was tightening round it. My heart pounded, my face was damp with sweat. And then I heard excited exclamations, and knew I had succeeded. The table (as I was told later) rose several inches into the air and hovered there for a breath-held moment before it thudded to the floor.

But the effort had left me with blurred vision, a terrible fatigue, a weakness in all my limbs. I felt my knees give way, and unthinking, thrust out a hand to recover my balance. To my dismay, I managed to topple the flimsy Japanese screen.

And that would have been disaster enough, as I stood revealed hot-faced and flustered in front of everyone. But worse — unimaginably worse — was gazing into the startled eyes of Tom Grenville-Smith.

He had arrived late, I suppose, and slipped in quietly. And now he was looking back at me with surprise and puzzlement, and something else that made my heart contract.

While Mr. Bertram was setting to rights the screen I fled into the refuge of HPB's bedroom, and would not come out till everyone had left. I'm not sure what Professor Lodge or our other visitors thought. Perhaps, as the Countess insists, they only thought me clumsy or unwell — for none of them, not even the Professor, has questioned Madame Blavatsky's latest miracles.

But Tom has guessed the truth. Or a part of the truth. I could see it in his face. What else can he believe but that I was assisting HPB in a cleverly stage-managed deception? In Tom's eyes, now, I am a shameless fraud who should answer for her misdeeds like any ordinary criminal.

CHAPTER TWENTY-FOUR

March 14

I am glad to be distracted by another of Alexandra's entertaining letters.

"Further adventures, chère Jeanne! When I left London I thought I had also left behind the world of spirits and séances; but I find they are not so easily escaped. I recently made the acquaintance of the Duchesse de Pomar, an elderly, eccentric Spanish lady, once married to a Scottish lord. The Duchesse and her circle are adepts of what in French we call *spiritisme*. The Duchesse hosts séances in her mansion on rue de la Université, and somehow, against my better judgment, she has persuaded me to attend."

As Alexandra describes it, the Duchesse's mansion is vast, and "*très magnifique*", with an enormous staircase of rose-coloured marble leading to the bedchamber where she receives her guests. A huge bed on a platform fills most of the room, and the ceiling is covered by hundreds and hundreds of painted angels circling round a golden star.

("How can she sleep with all those eyes looking down on her?" Alexandra wants to know.) There is also a chapel dedicated to Mary, Queen of Scots. The Duchess, who believes that she is the reincarnation of Mary Stuart, employs a medium to invoke the spirit of that ill-fated queen.

Alexandra writes, "You have attended one of these séances, Jeanne, so I need not go into detail. Suffice to say, there are the usual stage effects — fingertips touching round the table, flickering lamps, mysterious creaking and rapping noises. The medium directs some questions to the table — now possessed, one assumes, by the spirit of Mary Stuart — and the table obligingly raps out its answers, 'yes' or 'no'. If instead we ask questions of the medium, she replies with nonsensical babbling. All the while I am thinking to myself, how ridiculous this is! Mary Stuart was by all accounts a clever woman. Do we really become so stupid when we cross over to the spirit world?"

(Perhaps we do, if like poor Mary Stuart we have had our heads chopped off!)

"But yesterday," says Alexandra, "such a drama! From the table, usually so well-mannered, there suddenly erupted loud, disturbing noises. Everyone looked startled, and the medium, still in a trance state, began to thresh around in her chair. Then we heard a strange, hoarse voice, a man's voice, saying, to no one in particular, 'The arm of Karma reaches over you, impure couple! Your punishment is nigh. No longer defile this room with your presence!'

"*Quelle consternation*! All of us glanced furtively round, to see who might be looking the most guilty. Of course we wanted the spirit to name names, but that was all he had to say.

"Whose voice was this, and what was the purpose of the accusation? I have thought about it since, and I may have an explanation. Do you remember how Madame Blavatsky spoke of reanimated shadows, disembodied souls, who seek by whatever means to attach themselves to the living? They are sly and artful, these elemental spirits, and oftentimes malevolent. They like to play tricks on us, for no better reason than to cause hurt. When the medium went into her trance, invoking the spirit of the Queen of Scotland, she may have called up these mischievous elementals instead. And who knows? Perhaps these reanimated shadows can read our guilty thoughts — for which of us does not feel guilty about some real or imagined sin, and dread being found out?"

《 《 《

Alexandra's letter goes on for some pages to describe, with sly amusement, her further exploits among the Paris *excentriques*. But I have had to set it aside for a moment, for I found my hands trembling. What leaped to mind was the inescapable shadow of my cousin George — sly and evilly disposed in life, and, I could well imagine, equally malevolent in death.

CHAPTER TWENTY-FIVE

March 16

It was a whim of Fate, I think, that brought me to Lansdowne Place; and Fate that will close this chapter of my life. I know that very soon I must seek new employment. HPB is very ill. She has sworn off further entertainments until her health improves, and so has no need of my assistance in demonstrating her psychokinetic powers.

I think the Countess would like HPB to keep me out of charity, but there is little enough money coming in to support the rest of the household. With work on the final volume of *The Secret Doctrine* now all but set aside, and Mr. Mead and the Keightleys assisting with HPB's other obligations, there is little for me to do.

And that is not the only reason that I must leave Lansdowne Road. Over and over in my mind I have relived that moment when I stood revealed as HPB's accomplice. What must Tom think of me now? I cannot bear the thought of ever facing him again.

If only I were like Alexandra, who dearly loves a new adventure. But I have neither Alexandra's courage, nor her experience of the world, and I tremble at the thought of leaving this safe refuge.

March 30

This morning, while I was at the stationer's buying pens and a new journal book, I was approached by an odd-looking woman, very tall and gaunt, with jet black hair and a pale complexion. She was dressed in a long, loose-sleeved jacket encrusted with jet beads over a flowing black silk skirt, and a black lace shawl draped over that.

"Eet eez the young Scottish lady, eeze it not?" she cried, as she strode towards me like some long-legged, black-feathered bird of prey. "Tell me, how fares my dear Madame Blavatsky?"

And then of course I remembered that I had seen her at one of HPB's Saturday afternoons. It seems she is a psychic and medium, and she calls herself Madame Rulenska, though I believe the "Madame" is an affectation — when she forgets that she is meant to be Eastern European, her accent is broad East End London.

"Madame Blavatsky is not as well as we would wish," I admitted, "but she remains in good spirits."

"And is she still performing her parlour tricks?"

How dared she! Of course I leaped at once to HPB's defense. "They are not tricks! Everyone knows that she has special powers."

"Do we indeed. And a young lady assistant whose powers are perhaps — shall we say — even more special than Madame B's?"

I stared at her, cheeks burning, too flustered to reply.

"Dearie, your little performance may have fooled those West End ladies. But I too have special powers, and I saw exactly what was going on."

Hateful woman! I thought. (Though afterwards it occurred to me there was no disapproval in her voice.) In any event, I mumbled something about a luncheon appointment, hastily paid for my purchases, and fled the shop.

April 6

My dear Miss Jean Guthry,

Due to circumstanses arising from my practise of the psychic arts, I am taking the liberty of approaching you. That is to say, Miss Guthry, I find that pressure of business leads me to consider the timely employment of a qualified assistant. Should you in the near future find it nesessary or prudent to leave the employ of Madame Blavatsky, in view of the aforementioned sichuation I would be pleased to interview you.

I read this misspelled and convoluted message twice through before I understood that I was being offered a position; and I knew the time had come to make a decision.

"Oh my dear Jeannie," said the Countess Constance, when I told her of Madame Rulenska's letter. "And are you truly considering this offer?"

"I think I must." With what sadness and regret I spoke those words!

"If only I could tell you, stay here, Jeannie. We are all so fond of you, But with Madame B. so ill, I know you must think first of yourself, and how you will manage . . .afterwards."

We both understood the meaning of that half-whispered "afterwards." Someday soon — very soon, it seemed — we must all of us go our own ways, and Seventeen Lansdowne Road would be no more.

"I know very little about this Madame Rulenska," the Countess said. "Do you think she is a woman of good reputation?"

What could I say? The Countess knew as well as I that to the world in general, and to Madame Blavatsky in particular, all mediums were by nature disreputable.

"I suppose," I replied, "she is no worse than any other."

"Oh my dear," cried the Countess. "As bad as that? Promise me that if she is unkind, or the work is unsuitable, you will leave at once."

"I will," I said. But I knew that it was an empty promise. Life has offered the Countess the luxury of choice; while I must make the best of whatever Fate or accident sets before me.

April 12

I have replied to Madame Rulenska's letter. Tomorrow I will go to be interviewed at her house in Clerkenwell.

CHAPTER TWENTY-SIX

April 13

A s the railway plunged out of the daylight on its way to Farringdon Station, I imagined this descent into the underworld as a grim omen of what lay ahead.

Madame Rulenska's house is just off Clerkenwell Green, which sounded agreeable enough when she gave me the address, for of course I imagined the Green as a pleasant city square with trees and lawn, and perhaps some flower beds. What a disappointment! There is nothing green at all in Clerkenwell, as far as I can see. It is in fact a gloomy place of narrow streets and alleys, flanked by warehouses and commercial buildings, with two broad thoroughfares running through.

Shadowed by tall buildings, Madame Rulenska's house stands at the end of a treeless street. It looks a little down-at-heels — a front door in need of painting, lace curtains hanging limply behind windows with peeling frames.

Madame Rulenska greeted me at the door, and we went down a long narrow hallway into the parlour. It was stuffy and close, smelling strongly of potpourri, with a faint chemical undertone. I sat on an overstuffed sofa covered in wine-coloured velour, amid a profusion of embroidered satin and velvet cushions. On various small wicker tables stood a great number of china ornaments, souvenirs of holiday trips. The red velvet overmantel was decorated with gold braid and silken tassels, and on the walls were lithographs of courting couples and Grecian ladies in ornate gilded frames. There was, besides, a large potted palm, and on the floor a scattering of well-worn and faded Turkey rugs.

Over tea and stale digestive biscuits, Madame Rulenska described my duties.

She does not deal in the materialization of spirit forms, and hearing that, I was much relieved, not wanting to risk a second appearance of George's ghost. But she rattled off a list of other phenomena with which I am to assist: the usual knocks and raps (at which by now I am quite adept), the lifting and movement of furniture and other objects, and their sudden appearance out of thin air; and also the mysterious sounding of musical instruments. As well, Madame Rulenska practises clairvoyance, by which she means mind-reading, the viewing of messages in sealed envelopes, fortune-telling and the like. In all of these perfor-mances, I will be expected to assist. I have never shown any talent for fortune-telling or mind-reading (indeed, had I been able to foresee events, things surely would have gone better for me!) but I expect that Madame Rulenska has many tricks up her capacious sleeves.

She told me, "I have not had an easy time of it, you may be sure. My dear husband died of the cholera in sixty-four, when we were but two years married, and there was I, a widow, left to make my own way in the world, as best I can."

But is she a fraud, as most mediums are thought to be? When she had shown me to the sparsely furnished attic room where I was to sleep, and we were about to go downstairs, she turned, put her hand on my arm, and said, "My dear, I see there has been a great change in your circumstances. You have travelled far from home, have you not?"

Caught by surprise, I nodded.

"A journey that was connected in some way with a young man?"

I drew a sharp breath. *Surely she must mean George.* It was her next remark that made the hair prickle on my neck: "A young man who has served you ill and caused you much distress?"

How could she know this, when I have told not a soul in London why I left the Borders? And how much more has she learned about me? Not even Alexandra knows all of the truth, and I would trust her with a secret as I would with my life.

When we were finished the interview, Madame Rulenska showed me the room where the séances are conducted. It was much like the one at Crouch End — dark red curtains drawn across the windows, a heavy table surrounded by chairs; and a sideboard with a clutter of musical instruments; though I saw no cabinet like the one that Mrs. Brown had employed.

For better or worse, I have agreed to leave Madame Blavatsky, who for all her faults I have grown to like well enough; and become assistant to Madame Rulenska, who I suspect I will not like at all.

April 25

Today I gathered up my few possessions and said goodbye to Lansdowne Road. The Countess embraced me, suspiciously damp-eyed, and made me promise to visit whenever I could. The Messrs. Keightley shook my hand, solemnly, each in turn, and wished me good luck in "this brave new adventure." (I did not remind them that it was not I but Alexandra who seeks adventures.) As parting gifts Mr. Archibald has given me a box of fine vellum writing paper, and Mr. Bertram an ivory pen in its own case, "so that you can keep in touch." The Countess presented me with the first volume of *The Secret Doctrine*, saying with a smile, "When you have finished reading this, you must ask me for the second volume." (Alas, I fear that will not happen, for this massive book looks almost as daunting in print as did in manuscript.) And young Mr. Yeats, when he heard I was leaving Lansdowne Road, sent a copy of his first volume of poetry. It is called *The Wanderings of Oisin* (and a note is enclosed to tell me how it is to be pronounced — "Uh-sheen".) It's beautifully bound in rich dark blue, with letters in gilt — just as I once imagined my own books might be.

We none of us had the courage to tell HPB outright that my new employer was a medium, but of course she guessed. Sadly, she had not the strength for more than a token protest, though she condemned Madame Rulenska in no uncertain terms as a fraud, a jiggery-pokery artist and a flapdoodle. As I bent to kiss her cheek, as I had never dared to do until this day, she grasped my hand in one of hers, and whispered, "Take care, my child. Take care."

❝ ❝ ❝

April 26

At dinner last night I was introduced to Madame Rulenska's boarder, Mr. Rufus Dodds. He is a short, stout, sandy-haired, ruddy-cheeked gentleman of fifty or so. Madame Rulenska has told me privately that he used to be the Reverend Dodds, but had to resign his living in Berkshire because of inappropriate behaviour; and now devotes himself to writing a book on the history of Clerkenwell. Indeed, with his educated voice and kindly, somewhat abstracted air, I can easily imagine him as a country clergyman. I did not ask what that inappropriate behaviour might have been, for I do not wish to know.

Today at breakfast we found ourselves alone, and by way of greeting, as we helped ourselves to porridge, he asked "And how are you getting on with Madame Rulenska?"

"Well enough, I believe. She seems . . . " While I was still thinking how, tactfully, to describe my new employer, he remarked, "She is a fraud, of course — a charlatan of the first order."

I stared at him. "But . . . are you sure of that? There are things she told me, that surely she could not have known . . . "

Settling himself at the table, Mr. Dodds poured a cup of tea and added a generous helping of sugar. "Could she not? I am familiar with her methods, and I, who make no pretence to be clairvoyant, could be just as convincing. For example . . . Did she tell you that there was a young man in your life, and that he was somehow associated with a change in your circumstances?"

I nodded, feeling a faint chill as I recalled Madame Rulenska's words.

"Well then. I see before me an attractive young woman of marriagable age. For such a young woman, there is bound to be a young man somewhere in the picture. But this young woman is not London-bred, her speech is northern. For some reason our young lady has left home and has come to London. Supposing the young man in question is also from the north. Since our young lady is clearly sensible, of good reputation and, it seems, at present unattached, it is unlikely that they have run away together. On the other hand, she may have met someone in London. Whatever the case, I am safe enough in saying that there has been a change in circumstances. When I mention the young man I watch your face to see your reaction. If your expression is a happy one, I will hazard a guess that you've had an offer of marriage. If less than happy, the offer may have been declined. But should my mention of a young man cause you to look uncomfortable or upset, then I have gained another useful piece of information, and I will surmise that the encounter was not a pleasant one. You see?"

I was not at first convinced, but thinking it over, I believe that Reverend Dodds is correct. Madame Rulenska's talents are observation and intuition, not clairvoyance; and in that respect, she is every bit as clever as Dr. Conan Doyle's detective. But how gullible I was, how easily persuaded!

CHAPTER TWENTY-SEVEN

May 12

I n the fortnight past I have had few evenings to myself, but tonight there are no sittings, so I will take this time to bring my journal up to date.

The Clerkenwell household is small. Besides Madame Rulenska, Mr. Dodds and myself, there is the cook, Mrs. Bragg, and the maid-of-all work Milly. Mrs. Bragg's cooking runs to mutton, potatoes, cabbage and suet puddings, and not the spicy vegetarian dishes I grew accustomed to at Lansdowne Road. Milly is a plump, rosy-cheeked country girl of seventeen or so. She puts me so much in mind of the girls I knew in the Borders that I think we could be good friends; but Madame Rulenska makes it clear that as her assistant, I must keep the servants in their place.

No fashionable West End ladies, no duchesses or famous authors attend Madame Rulenska's séances. Her clients are people of modest means, widows of clerks and shopkeepers — chapel-goers with an unquestioning belief in an afterlife and the possibility of messages from beyond.

As she explained, though she sees her vocation as a caller-up of spirits, Madame Rulenska has also taught herself some simple stage conjurer's tricks. A part of my duties is to assist in displays of what she calls clairvoyance — the reading of things that are hidden. In one of her popular entertainments, a member of the audience is asked to write a series of numbers on a thick piece of card. Then I hold up the card so that the numbers are visible to the audience, but hidden from Madame Rulenska, who sits the front of the room. Madame R. hesitates for a while, as though the spirits (who supposedly are dictating the hidden numbers) are absent or inattentive. My task is to encourage her efforts, until finally, as revelation strikes, she reads off the correct numbers, one after another. This performance never fails to impress the onlookers, and convinces them of Madame's psychic powers, but the trick is absurdly simple enough once you know how it is done. All it requires is a good memory, and an ability to think on one's feet.

In Madame Rulenska's method, each number from 0 to 10 has a secret word assigned to it (and these words are changed from one performance to the next). For example:

Zero: Listen
One: Look
Two: But
Three: Is
Four: Ask
Five: What
Six: Yes
Seven: Please
Eight: Now
Nine: Tell

Ten: Madame

And so if the numbers on the card are 5, 2, 7, 6, 8, each sentence I speak to Madame must begin with one of the secret words, and the conversation might go something like this:

Me: "What (5) do the spirits tell you?"

Madame R: "Wait a moment, the message is not clear."

Me: "But (2) do you not hear what they are saying?"

Madame R: "Only very faintly. Wait, there is something . . . "

Me: "Please (7) try to listen more carefully."

Madame R: (With a touch of annoyance) "Really, I am doing my best.

Me: (Soothingly) "Yes (6) of course, Madame, we understand that."

Madame R: "(Brow wrinkled, listening hard) "Ah, that is much better!"

Me: "Now (8) are you able to tell us the numbers?"

Madame: "Yes, certainly. They are 5, 2, 7, 6, 8."

(Delighted applause)

I am becoming quite clever at this game, and I find that I enjoy the challenge. It is trickery, to be sure, but I think of a fairly harmless kind. I am much less comfortable with invoking the spirits of the dead. I feel it is very wrong to profit from a widow's bereavement, or a mother's desperate grief.

But now Madame Rulenska has added another stage trick. Each of our guests is asked to write a question on a card, then seal the card carefully into an envelope, and sign their name in ink across the seal. I collect the envelopes in a basket and take them out of the room — "to avoid any psychic interference," Madame Rulenska explains, obscurely. Then she leans back in her chair, breathes deeply, and drifts into trance. Our visitors, abuzz with anticipation, are left to chat among themselves.

After thirty minutes or so I return with the basket of envelopes. I choose half a dozen at random and pass them to their owners for inspection, asking them to confirm that the flaps are still firmly sealed down and the signatures intact. Then I gather up the envelopes and hand the basket to Madame Rulenska, now apparently deep in trance. She chooses an envelope, presses it with a dramatic gesture to her brow, and calls upon one of her spirits to read what is written inside. The odour of incense, oppressively strong in that close room, conceals the faint whiff of benzine that a sensitive nose might otherwise detect.

For that is how the trick, is done: with a benzine-soaked sponge, wiped over the front of the envelope until, briefly, the paper becomes transparent, and I am able to read what is written on the card inside. Then I take another, identical, blank envelope, write this question across the sealed flap, and mark it with the questioner's initials. That envelope, meant for Madame Rulenska's eyes alone, goes into the basket along with all the others.

There are two spirits whose task it is to answer questions. Running Wolf — so Madame Rulenska tells me — is an Iroquois chief from the wilds of Canada. He has a deep, gruff voice, and speaks in a peculiar sort of pidgin English. And then there is the Countess Violette, the shy sweet-voiced spirit of a French aristocrat, guillotined in the Revolution.

They take turn about manifesting themselves at our sittings. Both are very popular with our visitors, and no one seems to mind that their replies are too vague and general to be much help.

For example, this afternoon one of the ladies wrote on her card, "Where shall I look for my missing amber brooch?"

The Countess Violette, always eager to oblige, said, "Eet ees *très necessaire* to make a thorough search of your house, with particular regard to your bed *chambre*." (Which reply the lady received with a nod and a grateful smile — as though she could not have worked this out for herself.)

In another session a gentleman asked for investment advice, and was advised by Running Wolf to proceed with care, like a hunter in the forest, "for him who runs with heavy feet may lose much wampum."

For our afternoon sittings we draw the curtains and sit in half-light — an atmosphere of gloom being, I expect, more comfortable for spirit visitors than ordinary daylight. In the evenings, with the séance room plunged into darkness, Madame Rulenska's performances grow more adventurous, and she is finding new ways to make use of what she calls my "psychokinetic gifts". Besides the usual raps and knocks and dancing furniture, with my assistance she produces thrilling effects with "spirit lights". While our guests sit hands clasped in marvelling silence, I make hundreds of tiny points of light appear, and drift slowly round the room like luminous snowflakes, or fallen stars. "How strange! How wonderful!" I hear the astonished whispers, as the last of the lights float away, and audience begins to stir.

It is a trick that never fails to enchant and mystify. Our audiences leave with a comforting assurance that the spirit world exists, and is near enough at times to touch our own. No one suspects that in Madame Rulenska's bag of tricks is a vial of phosphorous oil, or that after the séance Millie comes with her broom to sweep from behind the furniture hundreds of tiny scraps of silk.

CHAPTER TWENTY-EIGHT

May 18th

With today's post, a troubling note from Alexandra:

Chère Jeanne,

I am writing letters tonight, because I find it impossible to sleep. Too little sleep, too little food, too much studying, that is what my mother says. My parents are urging me to return to Brussels, so that I can continue my studies in music. But Jeanne, I cannot bear the thought of life in Brussels. I would feel imprisoned. *C'est vrai*, I am exhausted, but it is a fatigue of the mind and spirit, not the body. These past months I have wandered down so many paths — exploring theosophy, occultism, esoteric religion — and lately, I confess, some paths better left undiscovered. Yet none of them have satisfied this restless longing — this search for a thing I can neither name nor describe. What shall I call it? Wisdom, understanding, the visionary experience, the light of divine clarity? In Paris, the City of Light, I thought to find it, but still it eludes me.

Write soon, *amie*. On nights like this my resolve fails, my search for knowledge seems like chasing after phantoms, and I am filled with a terrible *ennui*.

Alexandra.

❆ ❆ ❆

I did not imagine I would ever fear for Alexandra. She has always seemed so brave, so confident, in a way that I can never hope to be. But she spoke to me once about the fits of melancholia, or neurasthenia, that afflicted her sometimes in childhood, and now I think she may be slipping once again into that black mood of despair. And though Paris may be the City of Light, by all accounts it is a sinful place, where one as bold as Alexandra may easily be led astray.

❆ ❆ ❆

May 26

For some days now I have been unwell. My head throbs, my stomach churns, and I feel so dizzy at times that the room seems to spin round. Meanwhile, word has spread of Madame Rulenska's latest psychic feats, and we are now conducting séances as often as twice a day. I have always felt a little weak and disoriented after my performances, so that may be the cause of my unease. Yesterday before the séance I was drinking tea and chatting with our guests, hoping to glean some useful scraps of information for Madame Rulenska. While Mrs. Jones maundered on about her gallstones, and I nodded and smiled with pretended fascination, I came over so dizzy that my teacup slipped from my hand, and I all but fainted dead away. Madame Rulenska was alarmed enough to excuse me from my duties for the rest of the day.

Yesterday evening kind Mr. Dodds sat with me in the front parlour while I rested on the sofa, and he told me about the history of Clerkenwell. He is an excellent storyteller, and I found it all quite interesting.

I am glad I did not live in Clerkenwell in earlier times. "In the bad old days," says Mr. Dodds, "before the slums were cleared and the new roads built, it was the poorest and most dangerous part of London, the favourite haunt of pickpockets, thieves, murderers, and women of ill repute. But Miss Guthrie, what an abundance of history in these ancient streets! When you are better, I will show you the relics of the church of Saint John of Jerusalem, where the Knights Templar had their priory. And the house of the alchemist John Dee. Nowadays, Clerkenwell may be inhabited by watch and clockmakers and the occasional anarchist, but for centuries it was the refuge of outcasts, radicals and revolutionaries."

"And your book, Mr. Dodds? When do you think will it be published?" For in my recent experience, the result of all this research would be a tome as weighty as *The Secret Doctrine,* though, one would hope, more interesting to read.

"Published?" said Mr. Dodds. "Really, I had not thought of that. That would cost a great deal of money, would it not? The fun of all this, you see, is the investigation, the discovery."

Those could as easily have been Alexandra's words, or Tom's. Those two, I thought, would understand Mr. Rufus Dodds better than I ever could.

But the talk of books made me think of childhood hours I spent exploring the crowded shelves of my father's library, and my own long-ago dreams to become a writer. I could not have imagined, then, that my own life would take stranger turns than in any novel.

May 27

Today a red, oozing rash has come out on my hands. Though there is much I wish to write, it is difficult to hold a pen. In any event, my mind is in turmoil, after reading the letter that came in the morning's post.

> The Wethers,
> Fyfield Village, Wilts
>
> My dearest Jeannie,
> I hope you will forgive me for not writing sooner, but I have just recently returned from three months in East Africa with a zoological expedition. Yesterday I went round cap in hand to 17 Lansdowne Road to explain my lengthy absence, but to my great disappointment, I was told you had decamped. I have prevailed upon the Countess to give me your new address, and with your permission, I would like to call upon you, when next I am in London. I have much to tell you of my African adventures, and in return, you can tell me why you have abandoned leafy Holland Park for the drear wastes of Clerkenwell.
> In the meantime, in case you have not heard, there is much afoot at Lansdowne Road. First off, it seems that rumours of Madame Blavatsky's imminent demise were much exaggerated. The indomitable HPB, rebounding from the very edge of the abyss, is

recovered in both health and spirit. Her new friend Mrs. Annie Besant appears to have played a part in this. Have you had a chance to meet this paragon? She is a formidable feminist, a leader of strikes and organizer of unions, and HPB seems quite besotted with her. With my own astonished ears I heard her address Mrs. Besant as "my sweet Mango", and "my dove-eyed one." As you have guessed, I am endlessly fascinated by Madame Blavatsky's exploits. I suspect you are as fond of her as I am myself, and will be pleased to know that against all odds she is alive and well.

Still, what I am really writing to ask, Jeannie Guthrie, is when will it be convenient for me to call?

Yours, as ever,
Tom

CHAPTER TWENTY-NINE

May 28

I have read and re-read Tom's letter, and have slipped it between the pages of my journal, where I will see it each time I take up my pen to write. What a weight has been lifted from my heart! Surely he must understand what I am, and what I do — and yet he is able to forgive me, and I am still his dearest Jeannie.

But nothing escapes Madame Rulenska's inquiring eye. "Someone sent you a letter, I see. Was it the lover you came to London to escape?"

I hated myself for blushing. "You know very well I have no lover."

"So you say."

"And in any case, what makes you think it came from a man?"

She gave me a knowing smile. What a thoroughly disagreeable woman she is! "I have no trouble recognizing an envelope addressed in a gentleman's hand."

"You had no business to look at it all," I retorted. "But if you must know, it *is* a letter from a gentleman friend."

Her smile had turned into a smirk. "And what do you imagine a gentleman wants with you? A girl of no family, no place in society — who must use her wits to earn her keep? Mark my words, a gentleman only wants one thing from a girl like you, and you may be sure it isn't marriage."

"But he is not like that . . . "

"Don't be absurd. He is a man, is he not? And by the look of that envelope, one born with a silver spoon in his mouth. Make no mistake, they are all like that. And more to the point — who would wish to marry a girl possessed of unnatural talents — a freak of nature?"

I could feel my face flush with anger and indignation, but I knew I must not give her an excuse to dismiss me. As I fled towards my room I passed Mr. Dodds on the stairs, and he gave me a sharp look, saying, "My dear Miss Guthrie, what is wrong?"

"Why, nothing is wrong," I said, and made to slip past him.

"Then my dear child, why the look of one who has had the worst news in the world?"

And with that, a great lump rose in my throat; tears spilled over and rolled down my cheeks.

Mr. Dodds held out his handkerchief. "Come downstairs, you must tell me what is wrong, and if I can do anything to make it better."

"Now then," he said, as he sat me down on the parlour sofa and offered me a clean handkerchief. As I wiped my damp face I'm sure he noticed the state of my hands, for he gave me a troubled look. Embarrassed, I hid them in my lap.

"An acquaintance has written, and wishes to call on me," I said.

"And that is a cause for despair? There must be more to the story than that."

Wretchedly, I nodded. "Madame Rulenska says his intentions must be dishonourable."

"Well, my dear child, she would say that. Her business has flourished since you arrived. She would say anything in order to keep you here. But tell me, this young man of yours, is he proposing marriage? Or perhaps", he hesitated, "as Madame R. suggests, some other arrangement?"

"Certainly not. He is a friend, nothing more."

"And that is why you are weeping? My dear, I find all this dreadfully confusing."

"Because — Madame Rulenska is right, I am not fit to be his friend, still less to marry him. I have done a terrible thing, and may one day have to pay for it."

"You? My dear, I cannot imagine you doing anything very terrible."

And then — I cannot explain why I spoke as I did, only that Mr. Dodds is a kind old gentleman who wishes me nothing but good, and I am tired, and ill, and confused in my mind, and needed desperately to share the secret that weighs so heavily on my spirit. In any event, like water over a dam the truth spilled out — the truth I had not revealed to anyone, not even to Alexandra. In a headlong rush of words I spoke of what George had wished to do to me, and what I, in my fear and anger, had done to George. When I had finished, Mr. Dodds said quietly, "My dear, it seems clear that you inflicted a wound upon this fellow, which by the sound of it he richly deserved. But murder? Surely you have no reason to think that he is dead."

"But he could be. I have no way of knowing. There was a great deal of blood."

"But why assume the worst? That's the difficulty with not knowing — why I have never been fond of secrets. What people imagine can be far more shocking than the truth." I saw that sadness had crept into his eyes, and I guessed he was thinking of other secrets than the one I had just shared with him.

"But you must promise me, Mr. Dodds, you will not tell . . . "

"Of course I will not tell. Your secret is as safe with me, as if I heard your confession."

Which I suppose, in a way, he had. And foolish as it might have been, to reveal so much, I feel a little better for it.

What harm can there be in seeing Tom, when it would bring me so much pleasure? Madame Rulenska is I think a sad, embittered woman, who sees the worst in everyone. If she knew Tom, she would not say such things about him. He has always treated me as he would treat any friend and equal. And that is the true mark of a gentleman, my father always said: his manners are as good whether he speaks to the squire of the manor, or a shopkeeper, or a stable boy, or the chimney sweep.

I will send Tom a letter straight away, and say that he may call on me whenever he wishes, he need only write to let me know the day.

I hope, though, that when he comes I am in better health. This afternoon when Millie brought my tea, she said, "Why Miss, whatever have you done to your poor hands?"

"I don't know," I said. Millie took my right hand gently by the wrist and turned it palm-up, where the redness and oozing was at its worst. "'Pon my word, Miss, that's how my hands look after the spring cleaning. Have you been washing with carbolic?"

I shook my head. The only soap that I use is a soft rose-scented one that Countess Constance gave me.

"Well, I think you should have them seen to. Meantime, I have some lotion you can try."

Millie's lotion has helped a little, I think, enough that I was able to write to Tom, and make this entry in my journal. I thought for a long while about how I should address Tom, for I should not like him to think me too bold, but he has written "My dearest," and so I have gathered my courage, and (with what joy!) I have written, "My dearest Tom," and signed it "Your Jeannie."

But now there is a wretched headache behind my eyes, and all I wish to do is to sleep.

May 29

I am still tired and light-headed this evening. Madame Rulenska is thoroughly out of sorts, because she has had to conduct the afternoon séance without my help. I'd slept most of the morning, half-waking once when I thought I heard someone come into my room, but most likely that was Millie, who, bless her kind heart, is quite concerned about my health.

Just now I asked Millie if she would post my reply to Tom's letter, for I do not feel well enough to venture out.

"Not to worry, Miss," she said. "I saw it on the table, and I'll make sure it is sent."

And so tomorrow Tom will have my answer, and very soon, I hope, he will find his way to me in Clerkenwell.

Paris. 20 *mai*

Chère Jeanne.

I feel I should apologize for my last letter, which, I realize now, was as self-absorbed as it was doleful. I should instead have written to you of my encounters with the extraordinary M. Josephin Péladan and his followers, a group as entertaining as they are grotesque.

Have I yet mentioned M. Péladan? He is a true *extravagant*, who dresses in priestly robes and wears his bushy black hair and beard in the style of the ancient Assyrians. He plans to revive the mediaeval Order of the Rose-Cross of the Temple and the Grail, and wishes to be known as "Sâr Mérodak". (Sâr being a title of the Assyrian and Chaldean mages, and Mérodak a name for the planet Jupiter.) His Order, he says, will be a mystic fraternity bringing together the most enlightened artists, writers, musicians and thinkers. In the meantime he has written an extraordinary book called *How to Become a Fairy* — a feat which his female devotees are trying very hard to accomplish.

I was invited to tea at the home of one of his disciples, a lady of substantial weight and girth. I observed that she was tip-toeing about the room in a most peculiar fashion, lifting each foot high and then slowly setting it down. She must have sensed my curiosity, for she smiled and explained, "I am following the advice in the Sâr's book, and learning to become a fairy. One must practice walking with excessive lightness — with no more weight than a butterfly alighting on a flower. Thus the body, freed from gravity, is able to float on air."

I confess, Jeanne, though I am not often at a loss for words, I could think of no adequate response!

Hélas! What impulse draws me into this vulgar world of charlatans and pseudo-mages, these *mystificateurs* in their carnival finery, who prey on the deluded and hallucinated? And I think of you, Jeanne, possessed of genuine powers, but hidden away in Clerkenwell and wasting your talents in the service of a third-rate medium. Whatever would they make of you in Paris?

How I wish you could be here with me, my sensible Jeanne, to persuade me away from bad company and frivolous entertainments.

Alexandra

May 30

I feel a little stronger today, and thanks to Millie's ointment, the rash on my hands is fading. But Madame Rulenska will not excuse me from tonight's séance, for a spiritualist group is coming to see us perform.

May 31

It is difficult to write of what happened last night, as I scarcely understand it myself. Madame began with her usual repertoire of tricks — the raps and floating instruments and so forth — and moved on to the reading of secret messages, which went as well as usual. Then, as I was putting the envelopes into their basket, my feeling of lightheadedness returned, and I felt quite unsteady on my feet. But now it was time to dim the lamps, and call on Mlle Violette and Running Wolf.

Sudddenly, in that close, hot, incense-filled room, the world began to spin around me. I remember that I staggered, and grasped the back of a chair for balance. Figures appeared, cavorting round me in a mad quadrille. There was Mlle Violette, dancing headless and bloody in her wide silk skirts, and Running Wolf, a tomahawk in one hand and in the other, a dripping scalp. There were other faces, spirit faces, twisted with anguish, pallid and swollen and disfigured, fearful to look upon.

I must have cried out, for vaguely at a distance I heard a stirring and murmuring, a sound of bewilderment and concern.

And there was George, just as he had looked that day in the byre, blood dripping from his shoulder, his eyes filled with a dark and terrible intent. But I was not the one that he turned to with a look of murder — it was Tom who stood beside me, defenseless and unawares. It was Tom who was to suffer at George's hand, and I who must find a way to save him. We were in some other place, not Clerkenwell, the three of us suspended in that terrifying moment. My heart raced, nausea rose in my throat, pain lanced through my skull. My hands burned as though they were aflame, and I lifted them into the wind that gusted through the room. Things toppled and smashed. All around me I could hear the thud of falling objects, startled shrieks, the sound of splintering wood.

And then I was back in the ordinary world. Wide-eyed with astonishment and alarm, the spiritualist ladies were fleeing in disarray. Madame Rulenska, white-faced and furious, robbed for once of speech, stood staring: first at me and then at the circle of wreckage that lay around me like the aftermath of a storm.

"Well, that's a right mess you've made of things, in't it?" Her voice was loud and strident, all genteel pretensions fallen away. "You're a fat lot of use to me, my girl, if you're going to pull a trick like that!"

"I'm sorry . . . " I started to say.

"My dear, you've no call to be sorry." Mr. Dodds had come to stand in the doorway, teacup in hand, surveying the scene. "The fault is not yours, it is entirely Madame Rulenska's."

"Not her fault?" shrilled Madame Rulenska. "With the room in a shambles, and my customers run off in hysterics?"

"My dear lady, can't you see that you've made this poor child ill?"

"What, I've made her ill? What have I to do with it? If this how she means to behave, I've a good mind to put her out in the street."

Mr. Dodds' voice was quiet, but all at once it had a dangerous edge. "Like your last assistant, Madame?"

"Who, you mean Daisy? That went home to the country to care for her mother?"

"Ah, but it was not the mother that was sick, was it? It was poor little Daisy, whose hands were all red and raw from dipping them in benzine, and who fainted dead away from the fumes."

"Bollocks!" said Madame Rulenska. "Benzine's harmless enough, it's naught but cleaning solvent — I've used it often enough myself."

"But twice a day, six days of the week?" asked Mr. Dodds. "I think not. Nor, I think, are you sensitive to the fumes, as

Miss Guthrie clearly is. You may recall I warned you about Daisy. If you keep on like this, you'll have Miss Guthrie's death on your hands as like as not."

"And if you keep on interfering, I'll have the pair of you out on the street!"

Dear Mr. Dodds! I know that he is truly concerned for me, and is not afraid of Madame Rulenska's wrath. But Madame R. is as stubborn and self-centred as Madame Blavatsky ever was. She made no reply, just gave us both a venomous look and stalked out of the room, shouting for Milly to come and help set things to right.

CHAPTER THIRTY

June 9

Though I watch for the post twice a day there still has been no word from Tom. Surely by now he has had time enough to reply to my letter. Perhaps he is ill? I cannot believe that he has had a change of heart. But I have had another letter from Alexandra, which disturbs me almost as much as does Tom's silence.

> *Chère* Jeanne,
> I have been to visit my family in Brussels, and while I was there I paid my respects to my father's old comrade M. Elisée Reclus, who has retired to a pleasant house at Ixelles. In his old age he is as radical as ever, and continues to produce impassioned manifestos inciting the working classes to revolt. There in his pleasant suburban garden, or by his fireside late at night, political exiles, poets and free thinkers of all kinds grow drunk on cheap red wine and revolutionary fervour. And Paris, too, is delirious

with change, with the promise of revolution. You can smell it on the air, like a whiff of gunpowder.

Everywhere in the cafés are nihilists, anarchists, Marxists. Nothing is sacred, all things are possible. The artists too, and the poets, are caught up in the ferment, outraging the bourgeoisie and overturning stale conventions.

So do not be surprised, Jeanne, if I tell you that I have been visiting certain (almost respectable!) nihilist and anarchist salons. All my life I have been in a state of rebellion; and I have wasted too much time in the company of M. Péladan and his kind, with their absurd romantic fantasies.

Alexandra

June 15

My father always said that we must find our true purpose in life. His was a love of learning, and helping others to learn. No one at Lansdowne Road, least of all HPB herself, doubted for one moment that they had discovered their purpose. Mr. Dodds has his history of Clerkenwell, which he swears will occupy him for the rest of his days. Even Madame Rulenska has her questionable ambitions. And Alexandra — her purpose in life will be something grand and glorious, though I think she has not discovered it yet.

And as for me? I thought once, a long time ago, that I knew what I wanted out of life. I would scarcely recognize her now, that bookish child who dreamed of literary fame and her name in gilt. When I became a bondager, those high-flown ambitions shrank down to a simple need to be warm and dry, to have gloves for my hands and stout boots for my feet, to endure the winter and see the summer come again. At day's end I had a weeded field, a pile of mended sacks, the cattle fed; at summer's end the harvest safely gathered in. Purpose enough, I think, for most ordinary folk.

Alexandra writes of charlatans and mystifiers who prey on the deluded, but does she understand that is what I too have become? This life with Madame Rulenska is surely not what my father hoped for me, nor what I hoped for myself.

June 20

Mr. Archibald Keightley has written, enclosing notes from Mr. Bertram and Countess Constance with news of Lansdowne Road. He tells me that Madame Blavatsky is indeed much recovered, and the other day, persuaded by Mrs. Besant, she actually left the house, to attend the grand opening of a working women's restaurant. The Countess reports that for the restaurant opening the likes of Lady Colin Campbell, the Baroness de Pallandt and Mrs. Oscar Wilde were out in force, and HPB was in her glory. Oscar Wilde himself dropped by, and they traded barbs and witticisms in lively debate. And now, to the bemusement of the good Dr. Mennell, HPB is planning a summer holiday in France.

Reading Mr. Bertram's gossipy note, I realize how much I miss the lively, eccentric, world of Lansdowne Road. Mr. Willie Wilde, the journalist, has fallen on hard times, because (says Mr. Bertram, disapprovingly) he has wasted too much time in sporting clubs. Mr. Oscar Wilde is working on a novel which will undoubtedly cause a scandal. And there is more:

"Mr. Yeats has introduced his friend Miss Maud Gonne, an Irish lady with whom he is clearly in love. Miss Gonne is tall and very beautiful, has strong opinions and is said to be a revolutionary. We find her quite intimidating. She tells us that she has had occult experiences in which she takes leave of her body, gazing down at it from ceiling height. (HBP suspects her of using too much hashish.) One day Miss Gonne asked HPB if it was possible to be a Theosophist and also involved in politics. HPB advised her that she should do as she liked, and anyone who objected was a flapdoodle. Miss Gonne seemed pleased with this advice."

But from Tom, not a word. How foolish I was, to imagine for one moment that his intentions were serious, to think that our brief acquaintanceship could ever be more than that. Yet twice a day I listen for the post with a thumping pulse, tightness in my throat, and when there is no letter for me, it fair breaks my heart. I think of that long-ago night when we three bondagers, Edith and Nellie and I, gazed into the glass to see who we would marry; and for me there was only darkness.

June 24

Another week begins with another sad procession of heart-broken mothers and grieving widows, along with the usual assortment of curious onlookers. Every séance increases both Madame Rulenska's savings account, and my mood of melancholy. She refuses to let me give up the trick with the benzine, though now she allows me to work with a cloth over my face, and Mr. Dodds went to the chemist's and found me some india rubber gloves. But my illness has given way to malaise and boredom — what Alexandra would call *ennui et tristesse*. When Alexandra finds herself in such a state, her first instinct is to travel somewhere else. As she once admitted, she is quite fond of running away, not because she must, but simply because she can.

"What would they make of you in Paris?" Alexandra has asked. And "How I wish you could be here to persuade me from bad company." (To judge from her last letter, that company may be worse — and perhaps more dangerous — than she admits.)

If Madame Blavatsky, with her failing body and poor swollen limbs, can journey abroad . . . Is it possible? Could I simply run away? Again?

> *Chère* Jeanne,
>
> But of course it is possible! You must give your notice at once. What better time to see Paris, than in this summer of the Great Exhibition! We can be *touristes* together. I will show you my beloved Musée Guimet, and we will admire M. Eiffel's tower, which Madame Blavatsky so abhorred. We will "lean on the Pont de la Cité in front of Notre Dame and dream, with heart and hair to the wind." (That is my poor attempt at translating M. Paul Verlaine, a strange and disturbing and wonderful poet I have discovered of late.)
>
> I believe that *les Jourdans* may shortly have a room to let, and if not, you are most welcome to share mine. Also, until you find work you are not to concern yourself with money, for I am about to come into an inheritance, and expect to be embarrassingly rich.
>
> Write soon, *chérie*, and tell me when you expect to arrive.
>
> A.

July 5

I have confided my plans to Mr. Dodds, who said, "My dear girl, you are an employee, not a bondservant. Madame Rulenska may rant and rave, but she can hardly keep you here. And Paris? Well, I need not tell you that it is a perilous city for a young woman on her own. But you are a sensible young person, and so I am led to believe is your Parisian friend, Mademoiselle David. And as for the journey, what you want are a stout pair of boots and an up-to-date Baedeker's."

So on Mr. Dodds' advice I have purchased a copy of Baedeker's *Paris and Environs with Routes from London to Paris,* and have taken my boots to the cobbler to have them resoled.

July 7

I have given my notice. Madame Rulenska is not well pleased.

"What, are you daft? Leaving a good position in a respectable house? Scarpering off on your own, without so much as a by-your-leave, to some wicked foreign place?" She hovered over me, like a great black bird about to swoop. "You have no notion when you're well off, my girl. Don't I feed you and house you, and pay you good wages? Be bloody grateful I don't do materializations, like Mrs. Fisher down the street."

That thought made me shudder, for I've heard of the horrid trick Mrs. Fisher and some other mediums use to produce their ghosts and spirits: spewing forth lengths of white gauze from their stomachs and throats — or worse still, from other parts of their bodies. If Madame Rulenska imagined there was good money to be made, she would surely add it to her own repertoire.

Under that implacable black stare, I nearly lost my resolve. But I thought, Alexandra would not put up with this; and neither shall I. And so I turned and went straight upstairs to organize my belongings, leaving Madame Rulenska to shout at my retreating back.

PARIS

*. . . to embark on perilous travels and vast
undertakings . . . search for new perfumes,
bigger flowers, unknown pleasures.*
— Gustave Flaubert

*. . . in this street, in the heart of this magical
town . . .*
— Paul Verlaine

CHAPTER THIRTY-ONE

July 14

To travel by steamboat from London to Havre is much the cheapest way, though also very slow when one includes six hours of leisurely progress down the Thames, past wharves and warehouses and great fleets of anchored ships, past the Isle of Dogs, through Limehouse Reach and Greenwich Reach and finally out to sea.

Kind Mr. Dodds came down with me to the docks. "No place for a lady to venture all alone," he said, though in that noisy, bustling place, crowded with clerks and customs men and other travellers, I could not imagine I would come to any harm. As we said goodbye he pressed a pound note into my hand, "in case of unforeseen expenses," and would hear no refusal.

I have read that the Thames is the busiest river in the world, visited by thousands of ships from every faraway port, with every imaginable sort of cargo. Even the pungent dockside smells of tar and timber, sewage and coal-smoke, tobacco and turpentine and spice, hold the promise of adventure.

I think I must be a good sailor, for I did not feel at all queasy on the Channel crossing. Mr. Baedeker's guidebook says "Havre itself contains little to interest travellers", and this seems to be true, though there is a busy promenade from which one can look out over the water with its forest of masts, and a museum (not open today) with a fine collection of old coins and stuffed animals. But to find oneself in a great port city in a foreign country, on one's way to Paris, surely that is excitement enough for any traveller. The invaluable Mr. Baedeker mentioned an "unpretending" (meaning inexpensive) hotel near the centre of the city, and this is where I am spending the night, in a clean but very unpretending bed. Though a steamboat travels daily up the Seine to Rouen (fare only five francs) the trip is described by Mr. B. as "tedious", and another eight hours on shipboard is more than I wish to contemplate; and so instead I will spend a little more (fifteen francs forty-five centimes, third class) to travel directly to Paris by rail.

July 15

One hundred and forty-two and a half miles, seven and a half hours to Paris — every one taking me further from my old life, and all that is familiar. With Mr. Baedeker as my faithful guide, I am observing as much as I can of Normandy through the windows of the train, for who knows when I may travel this way again? We rolled past Graville ("with its curious church of the eleventh century") and then four miles on was the first station, Harfleur ("taken in 1415 by Henry V of England"). Now, after we cross a high viaduct and gather speed, there are villages, chateaus, a tunnel, another viaduct, and miles of pleasant countryside. After the junction with the Dieppe line comes, "a cheerful and picturesque district, abounding in factories," and finally we have arrived at the city of Rouen. Here, Mr. B. goes on a great deal about gothic churches and cathedrals which of course I shall not have the opportunity to visit.

More tunnels now as we cross the Seine, and stop at "several unimportant stations" along its banks. But here at last are the outskirts of Paris, and I glimpse M. Eiffel's metal giant rising against the skyline. Yet another tunnel and we are at the Gare St. Lazare, where Alexandra is to meet me.

❨ ❨ ❨

At first, swept up in that noisy, jostling crowd, I could not catch sight of Alexandra, and endured a moment of sheer panic. Could she have mistaken the day? Had she gone to the wrong station? Had she somehow been delayed? But no, there she was, small and trim and self-possessed in her sensible dark suit, waving and calling out to me.

"How well you look!" she declared, as she stepped back from my relieved embrace. "Clearly, travel agrees with you! First we are going to stop for a meal — I cannot subject you to the execrable Jourdan cuisine, your first night in Paris." And so we went to a café close by the station, to dine on oxtail soup and meat pies with mushroom sauce. Many of the voices I heard at the tables nearby were English, for Paris it seems is a wonderfully inexpensive place to live.

Alexandra's lodgings are much as she has described them, and the food as dreadful, though despite her earlier plans to lodge elsewhere, she has settled in quite comfortably. Luckily, as she has mentioned in her letters, there is a good, cheap restaurant nearby, and she has bought herself a few luxuries — an Indian rug, some bookshelves, a proper writing desk. I am to stay with her until a room comes available for me.

July 16

Once when I was quite young I found a book in Father's library called *Vie de Bohème*. I thought what a romantic life they must lead, those artists and poets in their draughty Paris attics, careless of all convention, existing only for their art. (Later on though, finding myself up to my elbows in a tater pit in a winter dawn, the notion of freezing in a Paris garret did not appeal to me so much.) But here in Alexandra's Paris it is summer, and the avenues are full of life and music and colour and I can scarcely believe my good fortune that I am to be a part of it all.

On the Boulevard St-Michel, students from the Sorbonne, artists, poets, bohemians of all kinds throng the pavements and the cafés. In the Latin Quarter no one ever seems to sleep. All last night, or at least until I fell into an exhausted doze, I could hear through my open window the rumble of cabs and the clamour of voices raised in lively (and often drunken) conversation and exuberant song. How far removed, this gaudy and exotic world of velveteen cloaks and flowing silk cravats, red berets and wide-brimmed hats and ostrich plumes and gypsy shawls and artist's smocks, from the sober black and grey of London. From Alexandra's window overlooking the street I watch the passing parade. Once I saw descending from a cab a woman so proud in her bearing, so elegantly gowned in her silk and pearls that I imagined she must be a lady of wealth and position, a duchess perhaps; but Alexandra says no, she is a woman of dubious reputation, one of the *demi-monde*, who has come to the cafés of the Boulevard St-Michel to mingle with artists and poets and perhaps with ruffians and thieves as well — for it seems that Boulevard St-Michel, like all of the Latin Quarter, has itself a dubious reputation. In the dead of night, when even the cafés had fallen silent, I woke to the sound of cursing somewhere outside in the street; but when I looked out all I could see was one sullen-faced woman in a ragged gown, hovering at the dark entrance to an alleyway.

July 17

Our landlady Madame Jourdan is a timid mouse of a woman, utterly devoted to her husband, whom she appears to regard with awestruck terror. She is responsible for all the cooking and housekeeping, as well as looking after the books of the Theosophist Society, even though she is not allowed to attend the meetings of the inner circle. At times it all becomes too much for her to manage, and Alexandra finds her hiding in the kitchen in tears. Both she and her three year old son look half-starved. Alexandra says she usually brings them back some buns and cheese whenever she goes to the market. From time to time Alexandra, who is afraid of no one, berates M. Jourdan for the way he treats his family, but it falls on deaf ears. M. Jourdan seems to exist solely on some higher plane. Madame Blavatsky would make short work of him, I think!

In these supposedly enlightened circles, one would expect women to be better treated, but sadly it is not so. Even as a bondager I felt less of a servant than poor Madame Jourdan.

July 18

Another fine summer morning spent exploring the stalls of used books and prints along the Seine. We bought some cheese and crusty bread to eat in the Luxembourg Gardens, which are close by Alexandra's lodgings, and then we wandered through the narrow, winding streets of the Quarter, full of odd little shops selling every sort of curiosity. I hope to sleep soundly tonight, for tomorrow we are to visit the *Exposition Universelle.*

CHAPTER THIRTY-TWO

July 20

I am not surprised that Madame Blavatsky so dislikes M.
Eiffel's tower. That metal colossus looming over the city
is startling to see and impossible to ignore. Alexandra tells
me that some of Paris's most famous writers and artists
protested its construction with an angry petition to the
city government, but to no avail. However Alexandra, who
because of her Oriental studies takes a longer view, says
"After all, it is only made of iron. In time it will simply rust
away, and fall to bits like Ozymandias."

In any event, it serves as a grand entrance to the Universal
Exposition, and passing beneath is like entering the gates
of fairyland. The exposition, spread out along the Champ
de Mars and well beyond, commemorates the hundredth
anniversary of the storming of the Bastille and the beginning
of the French Revolution. (I hoped there would be no guillo-
tines on display — to my relief there are not — though we
have heard there was a proposal, wisely rejected, to build
one thirty metres high.)

There is an endless and bewildering number of exhibits — more than 61,000, according to the official guide, "a gigantic encyclopaedia, in which nothing is forgotten." In the History of Habitation we saw a prehistoric house (rather like a tall, lumpy anthill), a Lapland and a Russian house, and homes of the ancient Egyptians and Phoenicians. We visited a Polynesian village, a Chinese pavilion, an Angkor Pagoda, a Portico of Ceramics, a display of antique Persian carpets. We rode on the *trottoir roulant*, the moving pavement, drank black coffee and ate pastries in a Moorish café, watched the Argentinean tango dancers, heard music played on gamelins by Javanese musicians, and opera played on Mr. Edison's phonograph machine. In a week, or a month, one could not hope to see and hear everything. We agreed to leave the galleries of Industry and Machinery and the Palace of Beaux Arts for another day; nor did we try to see Buffalo Bill and Annie Oakley in their "Wild West Show", for the crowds were far too thick.

Though it is advertised as one of the main attractions of the fair, what we enjoyed least was the *village nègre*, where four hundred native people from the African colonies are kept on display. "A zoo for human beings," said Alexandra in disgust. *"Quelle horreur! C'est révoltant!"*, and we quickly moved on.

By then my feet were starting to ache and my head buzzed. I swear that visiting an exposition is more work than thinning a whole field of turnips! But Alexandra, when she is in a mood to explore, has boundless energy.

As we walked through the "Bazar Egyptien", a voice behind us called out, "Mademoiselle David! *Quelle surprise!*"

We stopped and turned. Hurrying to catch up with us was a tall young man so fancifully dressed that he himself could have been placed on display. He was the very picture of the Paris dandy, with his carefully groomed and upturned moustache and his small goatee. Under an elegant cream-coloured suit he wore a silk waistcoat in shades of gold and rose and plum that might have been borrowed from an Oriental prince. His long flowing cravat was the colour of aubergines, and his jaunty straw hat, which he waved in greeting, had a bunch of violets stuck in the band.

"M'sieu d'Artois!" exclaimed Alexandra, looking faintly annoyed. She said, in French, "A surprise, indeed. Are you playing the part of tourist today?"

"In my own fashion," he replied.

"Jeanne." Alexandra turned to me and I looked up. (My attention had been distracted by the handle of the young man's ebony walking stick, in the shape of some fabulous beast with snarling jaws and ruby eyes.) In English she said, "Jeanne, may I introduce M'sieu Etienne d'Artois?"

M. d'Artois inquired politely whether we were enjoying our tour of the Egyptian Bazaar. He spoke in flawless English, though with a curious hint of a North of England accent.

"It is indeed most interesting, in *its* own fashion," said Alexandra, a trifle dismissively. "But there are limits to artifice. It cannot hope to replace the real experience of travel."

"But, my dear mademoiselle, *au contraire*! Why would you wish to endure the inconvenience and fatigue of travel, the unhygienic conditions, the indigestible food — the *bugs!* — when here you can enjoy the very essence of travel, the distilled experience? Nature is chaos, my dear Mademoiselle David. It is only through artifice we can experience it in civilized fashion. Permit me to quote from my favourite author: 'One can enjoy imaginary pleasures similar in all respects to the pleasures of reality'. Or are you perhaps not familiar with Monsieur J. K. Huysman's remarkable book, *À Rebours?*"

"I have heard of it, of course," said Alexandra. " I'm told it is the most wicked and perverse book ever written. It is much admired by the poets of my acquaintance."

"Wicked, yes. Perverse, without question. But therein lies its brilliance! A celebration of exquisite evil and divine *ennui*! But allow me to continue: 'Nature has had her day. There is not a single one of her inventions that human ingenuity cannot manufacture.' Thus, says Monsieur Huysman's hero, with a floodlit stage one can easily reproduce a moonlit forest, with papier-mâché a perfectly convincing rock. With silk or coloured paper one can reproduce the loveliest of flowers, without the inevitable withering and decay."

"I am advised," remarked Alexandra, "that M'sieu Huysmans, or his protagonist, says a great deal more than that, and none of it suitable for the ears of a respectable *jeune femme* . . . You will forgive our haste, M'sieu d'Artois, but we were on our way to see some paintings."

"I have seen them," said M. d'Artois. "A waste of time! Photographic realism, stale outdated salon art . . . scarcely so much as *un impressionniste*. Where are the Moreaus, where is Odilon Redon? These philistines have chosen to represent the dead past of art, not its future. But listen . . . " He dug into a trouser pocket and produced a hand-written card. "Next week in Montmartre there is to be a private showing of *Les Decadents*. Here is the address. There you may discover what true artistic vision, true genius, may aspire to."

"Perhaps we shall." Alexandra tucked the slip of her paper into her bag. "Au 'voir, M'sieu d'Artois."

"Let us stay till after dark," said Alexandra, "and see the lights come on." And so we had dinner in an outdoor restaurant, where we ordered cheese soufflés and a bottle of white wine, and were serenaded by a string quartet.

"And what did you make of Monsieur d'Artois?" Alexandra inquired, as she spooned up the last morsel of her baba à rhum.

I was not sure how I should reply. In truth, M. d'Artois's manner, and his strange talk, had made me quite uncomfortable. But Alexandra was a woman of the world; perhaps she did not find him so disturbing.

"He seems very . . . sophisticated," I ventured. "I suppose in that way he is a typical Parisian."

Alexandra burst out laughing. "*Au contraire*, Jeanne! He is not at all Parisian! That too is artifice. His real name is Albert Henslow. He is the son of a factory owner in Leeds. He is quite depraved, and a terrible poseur, and reads too many of the wrong sorts of books. He is not a person you would wish to know."

And yet I noticed that she did not throw away the slip of paper he had given her.

While we dined the summer twilight had deepened, and now all at once thousands of twinkling, glimmering electric lamps lit up the bridges and gardens and pavilions and the tower itself, transforming the exposition grounds into a festival of light.

It was nearly midnight, and both of us a little tipsy from the wine and baba à rhum, when at last we went in search of a cab to take us home. Said Alexandra, as we turned to gaze back at the tallest building in the world, enveloped in magical, otherworldly light, "Perhaps there is some place for artifice after all."

CHAPTER THIRTY-THREE

July 22

Today Alexandra seems oddly quiet, even a little melancholy, whereas only a short time ago she was filled with tireless energy. I am just now discovering that she can be a creature of shifting moods. What excites her enthusiasm one week, she is apt to find dull and tedious the next. There is a restlessness in Alexandra that is not I think in my own nature. Experience has taught me it is best to be content with the present — or at least resigned to it — because the future may hold something even less to one's liking. But for Alexandra there is always the tantalizing possibility of new adventure around the next curve of the road.

In this fine summer weather we are much out of doors, walking in the Luxembourg Gardens and wandering along the Seine. We have visited Notre Dame Cathedral, and I am promised, soon, a whole day at the Louvre. At dinner hour we eat cheap restaurant meals of *omelettes* and beans and crusty bread, and then as a rule spend the rest of the evening quietly at home. We record the day's events in our journals, and Alexandra writes long letters as well, to friends in London and Belgium.

I have had a letter of my own from Lansdowne Road, to say that Madame Blavatsky, on holiday at Fontainebleau, is still enjoying her remarkable return to health. Pleased as I am to hear the Countess's news, there is another letter that I look for, still, with a faint and foolish hope, when the time is long past to set that hope aside. Still, every day in Paris is filled with new experiences that leave little time for such vain regrets.

July 24

Last night Alexandra declared that she was weary of staying in, and so we went out to the nearby Café du Luxembourg to meet some of her friends. We sat down at a round marble table in a large dim room smelling of coffee and cigarettes and beer. I looked around. At other tables, and on long green sofas along the wall, stubbly-chinned young men in the student uniform of slouch hats and threadbare jackets talked and smoked and played at dominoes. I felt a little uncomfortable at first, seeing that for the moment we were the only women in the place, but Alexandra seemed very much at home. Almost at once, we were joined by three of the young men, who brought with them their tankards of beer and drew up chairs without an invitation.

Alexandra introduced me round the table. Two of the young men, Pierre and Gabriel, were students at the Sorbonne. The third, called Edouard, was older than the others — a heavy-set, shaggy-bearded man of thirty or so, wearing a shabby black jacket, heavy boots and workman's cap.

"Edouard writes for *Le Révolté*," said Alexandra, and I could tell from Edouard's expression that I was meant to be impressed.

But what was *Le Révolté*? I had no notion of how I should reply. Alexandra came to my rescue.

"That is the famous revolutionary newspaper in rue Mouffetard, owned by my father's good friend Elisée Reclus."

"Famous, yes," said Edouard. "The very nerve centre of Parisian anarchy — at least, according to the police. And our editor, Jean Grave, is the coordinator of all the Paris groups."

This mention of the police was discomforting, to say the least. Alexandra had written of visiting "almost respectable" anarchist salons. But how respectable can these anarchists be, if they are so well known to the police?

But Edouard was eager to tell me more about his newspaper. "We have some of the best writers in Paris contributing articles, and some of the best-known artists illustrating our pages. What we must do now, is to engage the interest and involvement of the workers."

"Mlle Guthrie has been a worker," said Alexandra.

Edouard regarded me with greater interest. "Indeed? A factory worker, mademoiselle?"

I shook my head. "I worked on a farm. In the Scottish Borders,"

"Ah, so . . . then you of all people will be sympathetic to our cause."

"And what cause is that?"

"But of course, to bring together the workers, the artists and the intelligentsia in collective action, to destroy the established order."

"The established order?"

"The people in power, mademoiselle. The propertied classes. The bourgeoisie. Tell me, for whom did you work, on your Scottish farm?"

"I worked for the steward."

"And who did the steward work for? Who was it owned the land?"

"Why, Mr. Murdoch."

"And labouring in those Scottish fields, did you and your fellow workers not dream of overthrowing this Mr. Murdoch, of seizing the land and sharing it for the common good?"

This struck me as a very odd idea. Why would we wish to overthrow Mr. Murdoch, who seemed a decent, God-fearing man, and a fair employer? He paid our wages on time, sent for the doctor when we took ill, and allowed us whatever holidays were due to us. And as for his eldest son and heir — though we women might amuse ourselves with idle dreams of marrying the handsome Robin Murdoch, overthrowing him was the last thing in our minds.

Edouard, warming to his subject, signalled for more beer. "This is what we at *Révolté* are working towards, mademoiselle — the cause to which we have dedicated our lives. To make the workers conscious of their position, and their power, to help them to rise up and throw off their chains."

The smoke from his cigarette, billowing across the table, made me cough, and I was getting a headache. Then one of the students, Pierre, I think, decided to take issue with Edouard's revolutionary ideas, and the two of them began to argue in such rapid and impassioned Parisian French that I could not possibly keep up.

Alexandra, with a tankard in one hand and a cigarette in the other, said little but seemed to be enjoying the debate. Finally, to my great relief, she announced that it was time for us to say goodnight.

I did not sleep well last night. I kept turning over in my mind the remark that Edouard had made about his employer being known to the police. I realize now that Alexandra is far more familiar with these people than her letters had suggested.

Is it possible that Alexandra is also known to the police?

July 26

Alexandra is restored to her enthusiastic, inexhaustible self, though a little too much so, perhaps, for we have stayed up every one of these past nights till well after midnight. I have woken in the small hours to find her still at her desk, writing in her journal by candlelight. She seems quite untroubled by lack of sleep, though our late hours leave me feeling out of sorts.

I know that I should be seeking employment — it should not be difficult to find work as an English tutor, as do many other young English people living in France. I fear that if I do not soon find respectable work, I might have to exploit my other talents, as I did in London; and that is something I wish to avoid at all costs.

But Alexandra makes light of these worries, saying that she has plenty of money and little on which to spend it. "Time enough to seek work," she says, "when this glorious summer is ended, and we are kept indoors by cold and rain."

July 28

It's three AM by Alexandra's little clock, and I am still awake, so rather than continue to toss and turn, I have taken out my new journal to write of this night's expedition. (Alexandra has given me a very handsome one with a dark red cover and a pattern of lilies on the front.)

"If you have not been to the cabaret Le Chat Noir," said Alexandra, "you have not seen Paris." And so we set out this past afternoon for Montmartre, meaning only to stay until the supper hour. But Alexandra's eagerness for adventure has carried us into a place where I would never have ventured on my own, and where I saw and heard things that have left me sleepless and overwrought.

The afternoon began pleasantly enough as we climbed the steep streets and stairs of Montmartre in late afternoon sunshine. Le Chat Noir is as much art salon and theatre as it is cabaret. The ground floor is decorated in a sort of mediaeval theme, with a stained glass bay window and a lot of imitation tapestries. The walls are entirely covered with paintings and drawings by Montmartre artists who have been refused by the academic galleries, and so display their work in the cabarets instead.

Along with the artists, well-known writers like M. Emile Zola and M. Alphonse Daudet frequent Le Chat Noir, as well as composers of music like M. Claude Debussy, and poets "both famous and infamous", as Alexandra says. The owner, M'sieu Salis, has introduced a piano, in defiance of the peculiar law prohibiting music in cabarets; and this flavour of disreputability has greatly added to the Chat Noir's popularity. (Especially, says Alexandra, among the fashionable and well-to-do who like to imagine themselves a little wicked.)

We had arrived, it seemed, at *'l'heure verte*", which is two hours, really, from five to seven PM. As we looked for a quiet corner table not too close to the illicit piano, Alexandra explained why this was known as the green hour: it was the time of day when the poets and artists of Montmartre were fond of sipping absinthe. As for Alexandra and me, we were content for the moment to order coffee and madeleines.

On the floor above is a famous shadow theatre (according to the menu, which I confess to have stolen, "admission is included in the price of beer") and so we went upstairs to see a play called *Carnaval de Venise*, with gondolas and Venetian palazzos lit up by lamps behind a screen.

Downstairs, later, there were performances by the *poet-chansonniers* — the poets both famous and infamous. The owner, M. Salis, very much the showman, introduced each one of them by saying, "Silence, listen to him (or her), a genius is in your midst!" Gabriel Montoya and Yvette Guilbert, who are famous all over Paris, sang tonight to much applause; but lesser known poet-singers also had their chance to take the stage. Most of the songs were very down to earth, about life in present day Paris; but one pale, gaunt young man dressed all in black sang a strange lament in the manner, Alexandra says, of M. Baudelaire.

Here, *en anglais*, are some of the words as well as I can remember them, translated with Alexandra's help:

You come to me at twilight
under the broken walls of the Old City,
where the Aubergine's dark waters
sigh like tattered silk.
You come to me from the shadows
under a bruised sky, heavy

with unshed rain,
Your small feet make no sound
on the lichened stones.
I feel on my throat
your insubstantial touch,
your chill sweet breath.
Our days apart
are a fever-dream, a torment,
each meeting
a small exquisite death.

The song reminded me a little of Alexandra's acquaintance Etienne Henslowe d'Artois. It was, I thought, just the sort of thing he would appreciate. I was also thinking that the hour was growing late for two young women who must travel home through the dark Paris streets — especially in a district with Montmartre's unsavoury reputation.

But then: "Mademoiselle David! Mademoiselle Guthrie! How very pleasant to find you here!"

I looked up and there, quite as though I had conjured him up, was M. Etienne d'Artois himself, resplendent in an evening suit of claret coloured velvet. And now he was settling in at our table, clearly inclined to chat.

"What was your impression of that last singer, Mademoiselle Guthrie? An interesting performance, was it not?"

"His voice is pleasant enough," I agreed. "But did you find the song a little . . . " I hesitated over the right word — "a little morbid, perhaps?"

"Morbid! *Précisément!* That is exactly what I should have said — a delicious morbidity! The perverse beauty of the fevered imagination!" ("Perverse", I do believe, is M. d'Artois's favourite word.)

Summoning our waiter, he asked "Is this your first visit to Montmartre, mademoiselle?"

I nodded.

"And you are drinking coffee? *Non, non*, that will simply not do." And over our faint protests, he ordered absinthe.

"*Voila, mesdemoiselles*," said M. d'Artois, "Elixir of wormwood — the green fairy!" The waiter had brought us three tall footed glasses, each with a portion of pale green oily liqueur, along with three long slotted spoons, a bowl of sugar cubes and a jug of ice water.

M. d'Artois led us through the ritual, resting the spoon over the glass and placing a sugar cube in its bowl, then pouring cold water over the sugar, until the liquid in the glass turned cloudy.

I did not much like the sound of "elixir of wormwood", and besides, I have read that absinthe drinking can drive you mad, but I took a cautious sip for politeness' sake. Tasting of anise and bitter herbs, it was not as unpleasant as I had feared, but there is little danger that I will become addicted to it.

"Now," said M. d'Artois, the absinthe ritual completed, "since Montmartre is a new experience for you, allow me to tell you a little of its history, which is delightfully bizarre."

Alexandra, sipping her absinthe, listened with an air of tolerant amusement.

"You must understand that Montmartre has always been a place of magical power, a refuge in every age for mystics and visionaries. Once, Montmartre was a sacred site for the Druids, and under Rue La Vieuville there are temples dedicated to the Roman gods. Saint Denis, the Bishop of Paris, was beheaded here, and according to legend, far from being discouraged by this, he picked up his head and carried it with him for several miles, while continuing to preach a sermon."

Alexandra caught my eye; the corners of her mouth twitched.

M. d'Artois forged on: "And then during the great uprising, the Commune of 1871, hundreds of revolutionists hid in the chalk mines of Montmartre and were forever entombed there, when the Army of the Republic dynamited the exits."

It's true, I had smiled at the absurdity of the headless bishop. But "delightfully bizarre"? Is this how M. d' Artois thought of those hundred of dying citizens, trapped by a cruel army in a place with neither light nor air? Was all wickedness, all human suffering, mere entertainment?

I had no wish to hear more. I turned away, on the pretext of examining a group of Paris street scenes on the wall behind us.

"You admire the Impressionists, mademoiselle?" Alas, M. d'Artois's attentions were persistent.

"They are new to me," I said, but yes, I find them interesting."

"But nonetheless, they appeal to a bourgeois sensibility. They are all surface — the play of light and colour. These are not artists who penetrate to the mysterious centre of the human soul. We must introduce you to the *Symbolistes*, mademoiselle — to the art of dreams, of visions, of the imagination *fantastique*." When M. d'Artois speaks, I always feel that he is quoting someone. He does not strike me as a gentleman with a great many original ideas. And though I did not say so, I am well content with paintings full of light and colour. There are things that lurk in the shadows that I do not care to discover.

He turned to Alexandra. "Mademoiselle David, have you by chance had an opportunity to view that private showing that I mentioned?"

"Oh yes, the Decadents," said Alexandra. "You were kind enough to give me the address . . . one day soon, perhaps."

"But what better opportunity than tonight? The studio is only one street away."

"But the hour is late," said Alexandra.

"*Mais non*, it is not a salon, it is the artist's studio, and like all true artists, he never sleeps at night."

I looked across the table. *Alexandra, please say no.* It was not merely the late hour that prompted that wordless plea. More and more, I found M. d'Artois's company unsettling; and some instinct made me fear where this adventure might be leading us.

CHAPTER THIRTY-FOUR

July 29

This morning both of us slept late. Last night, as M. d'Artois led us out into the dark streets of Montmartre, sleep seemed the furthest thing from Alexandra's mind.

The studio of the artist Jacques Gautier occupies the topmost floor of a tall, thin, ivy-covered house. We followed M. d'Artois up the stairs in single file and finding the artist's door flung open, stepped through into a long narrow room. On this close summer evening it was horribly hot and airless. The smell that greeted us seemed compounded of coffee, candlewax , cigarettes, turpentine, and unwashed clothes; to which was added, now, the musky sweetness of M. d'Artois's perfume.

There was another visitor in the studio when we arrived — a gentleman who appeared to have been seized by a painful fit of coughing. I could not see much of his face, as he was bent over in his chair with a handkerchief pressed to his mouth. The artist, who hovered anxiously nearby, was a pale, lean young man with luminous dark eyes and an earnest look. He acknowledged us in an offhand way,

gestured to the bottle of wine on the table, and left us to
our own devices.

The studio was much as I had imagined it would be,
from my long-ago reading of *Vie de Bohème*. There was
a single narrow window behind a length of black velour,
a velvet *chaise longue* that was ripped across the back
with the horsehair stuffing spilling out; a bench covered
with an elaborately embroidered altar cloth; some oddly
shaped candlesticks like twining serpents; a carved ebony
mask — African, I think — and a stained and fraying India
rug over bare floorboards. A folding screen in one corner
likely concealed the artist's bed. In the centre of the room
was a table splashed here and there with dried paint and
littered with what looked like the evening's unwashed
supper dishes. Elsewhere, hanging on the walls or propped
against them, on easels or leaning against a chair, were
dozens of paintings for which the only possible word was
macabre.

No cheerful Paris street scenes here — instead there
were crumbling pillars wound about with creeping plants
and hothouse flowers; a wild-eyed Salome, reduced to a
single veil, holding up the gory head of John the Baptist;
dragons and skeletons and sphinxes; exploding suns; and
beautiful drowned women, their long pale hair adrift like
strands of weed.

M. d'Artois stepped aside to allow me a better view
of spectral figures dancing on a row of coffins. "*C'est
intéressant, n'est-ce pas?*" he said approvingly. "The art of
melancholy slipping into madness" — which struck me as
an apt enough description.

Behind me, the hacking cough continued. The
unfortunate gentleman seemed in some distress. I turned to

see M. Gautier offer him a glass of wine, which he drained in a single gulp.

On one wall, half in shadow was a large untinted photographic reproduction. My gaze distracted by M. Gautier's acid greens and saffrons, his aubergines and brassy reds, I'd failed to notice it at first. Now I went to examine it more closely. In the background I could see the pinnacles and archways of a gothic palace or cathedral; mysterious towers half-hidden in vegetation; and on the far horizon, rocky crags. In the foreground, fantastic images were layered one upon another, bewildering to the eye: naked goddesses mounted on bulls and hippogryphs, a queen in the crown of Charlemagne stroking a unicorn's head, a serpent-headed goat; as well as fairies, angels, witches, and all manner of fabulous birds and beasts. I could have spent an hour examining it and still found more details to discover. Our host's own canvases by comparison seemed garish and inexpert.

"I see you are admiring M'sieu Gustave Moreau's famous picture," said M. d'Artois. "*Les Chimères* — a masterpiece of artifice and invention. He never finished it, you know. To portray all of myth, all of history, all of religion — what artist is equal to such a task?"

And I, who know so little of art, could only murmur, "It's beautiful, and very strange, and I think quite frightening."

"Just so. A journey through the haunted forests of the imagination. The reflection of our dreams, our terrors and our innermost desires."

Even in black and white, the picture had the power to mesmerize. If one looked too long, one had to tear one's gaze away. I could well imagine that beyond the distant mountains of that never-to-be- finished painting lay a still more marvellous and seductive country existing only in the artist's mind.

I was raised to believe that in this life, at least, there is only one reality, and that is the world of ordinary experience, that has no place for unicorns and hippogryphs. But all that has happened these past months has tested that belief. If we believe in Heaven, is it so impossible to believe, as spiritualists do, that other worlds exist above and beyond our own? At that moment I remembered a long-ago moment in a London bookshop, seeing through an artist's eyes a marvelous tropical world I had never visited, and likely never would. I had accepted those drawings not merely as vivid works of the imagination, but as a true record of the artist's travels. How much harder, then, to imagine that in some world invisible to the untrained eye, M. Moreau's chimeras were real?

"A world of nightmares," remarked Alexandra, coming to join us.

M. d'Artois looked a little affronted. "I take it, mademoiselle, you are not an admirer of M'sieu Moreau's work?"

"It reeks of romanticized despair," said Alexandra. "And besides, it is far too cluttered. I am not surprised M'sieu Moreau did not manage to complete it. Your author M'sieu Huysmans, of whom you think highly, has described it well: "A soul exhausted by secret thoughts . . . Insidious appeals to sacrilege and debauchery . . . "

"Why, mademoiselle, *quelle surprise*! I did not imagine you were so familiar with M'sieu Huysman's books!"

"And who in Paris is not?" said Alexandra.

It is unlike Alexandra to be so critical, even in the presence of the frequently annoying M. d'Artois. I wondered if something in M. Moreau's dreamworld affected her more than she cared to admit.

Just then the coughing gentleman put away his handkerchief, and M. d'Artois gave a cry of happy recognition.

"*Mon Dieu!* Can it be?"

The gentleman glanced up with a somewhat absent expression.

"Mademoiselle David, Mademoiselle Guthrie, allow me the great honour of introducing you to the most famous poet in France, M'sieu Paul Verlaine."

Alas, the most famous poet in France, on close inspection, appeared to have fallen on hard times. His graying beard was shaggy and untrimmed. His eyes were bloodshot, and his face had an unhealthy yellowish tinge. The high dome of his forehead was slick with perspiration. There were stains on his jacket, a button was missing, and a shoulder seam had given way.

"M'sieu Verlaine," M. d'Artois addressed the poet in his rather affected French, "Do you remember when we met one night at Le Chat Noir, and you read from your *Poèmes saturniens*?

In a palace of silk and gold in Echbatan
Beautiful demons, youthful Satans,
To the sound of Mohammedan music
Dedicate their five senses to the seven sins.

M. Verlaine dismissed this intrusion with an irritable shrug. "A young man's fantasizing. In fact, a piece of derivative garbage . . . " And waving away M. d'Artois's protests, he added, "It is true, I was once a genius. But now I am old and sick, and there will be no more poems."

"Indeed," cried M. d'Artois, "you are not at all old; you are in your prime!"

"But let us not pretend for courtesy's sake, M'sieu, that I am not ill. You see the evidence before you. I am a drunk, and in consequence have destroyed both liver and stomach." He held out his glass for more wine, obligingly poured by M. Gautier. "Let us add to the list, diabetes, and also a shrunken heart, which you will agree is a tragic condition for a poet. And from sleeping rough in Paris slums, I have developed rheumatism."

M. d'Artois was clearly at a loss for a reply. Alexandra, adroitly rescuing the conversation, said, "I possess a volume of your poetry, M'sieu Verlaine, I read it often, with the greatest pleasure. M'sieu d'Artois has his favourite among your lines — I have mine:

In a street, in the heart of a city of dreams,
that seems like a place where you have already been,
an instant at once very vague and very clear . . .

For a moment M. Verlaine's haggard, dissipated features softened. "You do me honour, mademoiselle — but tell me, have you ever travelled to that city of dreams?"

What a curious question, I thought. But Alexandra replied, in all seriousness, "Not I, M'sieu. Not yet. But I have known those who have found themselves, that is, a part of themselves, in a place they had not meant to go, which was unknown to them: a place they could only say was 'elsewhere'."

"Ah yes, I have done that," said M. Gautier. "Many times."

"But we are not speaking of drugs," said M. Verlaine. "Is that not so, Mademoiselle David?"

"No, nor of sleep, in the ordinary way," said Alexandra. "I once spoke to a woman who had made this kind of spirit voyage. All the while she was sitting in her chair, in a Paris drawing room, in the presence of two friends. She was not asleep, she had taken no drugs. Yet she slipped into an unconscious state, as though she had been given anaesthetic. All her senses were muffled, she could not move. And then she saw in the distance her other self, her spirit double, attached to her body by a thin, hazy cord."

"And where did she go, this other self?" asked M. d'Artois, clearly fascinated.

"She said, to a country that seemed familiar to her, though it was a place where she had never been."

"And who is to know," said M. Verlaine, "which is real, and which is not — the Paris drawing room? Or the city of dreams? That is a question for which I have long sought an answer. And you, Mademoiselle David — I think you have puzzled over it as well."

Alexandra, oddly, did not reply. I could not have guessed, at that moment, what was in her mind.

It is a puzzle for me as well, the nature of this place called "Elsewhere" — this paradoxical country, unknown and yet familiar, where we travel not in body but in spirit. For M. Verlaine it is the magical city he has only visited in dreams. For Madame Blavatsky surely it must be an otherworldly version of the Himalayas, a treasure house of ancient knowledge guarded by Tibetan sages. And as for Alexandra — I think she would see it as a dazzling instant of illumination, when all the mysteries of this world and the next are finally revealed.

By the time we were ready to be escorted home by M. d'Artois, M. Paul Verlaine had finished a second bottle of the artist's cheap, vinegary wine. His speech was slurred, his voice thick with drink and despair as he muttered, as though to himself, "I have squandered my art as I have squandered my life, searching for that other country."

And then, as we turned to go down the stairs at the end of that long, extraordinary day, he called after us, "You and I, we could search together, Mademoiselle David. My good friend Gautier will know where to find me."

CHAPTER THIRTY-FIVE

August 11

I have moved into a room of my own, *chez Jourdan*, now that one has come available. It is small, stuffy and sparsely furnished, but also very cheap. Alexandra advertised at the university and found two students who are willing to pay me for twice-weekly English lessons in the Jourdan's parlour, and so I am able to manage my rent and also send a little money to my mother. Still, this situation cannot continue. I must look for regular work.

I wonder what my mother makes of the Paris postmarks when she receives my letters. How I wish I could give her my address, so I could have news of home! Little Robbie will be walking and talking now, and Margaret starting school. I cannot bear the thought that I may never see them again.

Meanwhile, I am becoming quite worried about Alexandra. She has grown very thin and pale, and there are dark shadows under her eyes. She eats little, sleeps late, and complains sometimes of stomach ache. I cannot put out of my mind that disturbing letter I received in London, when she wrote of her spiritual exhaustion, her *ennui.* Now I believe it is happening again — I see with deepening concern her mood of melancholy, her loss of appetite, her look of weary disillusionment. Even on these perfect summer days she will sometimes choose to bide in her room, writing page after page in her journal. She is much more devoted than I, in the habit of daily entries; though when I see how she furrows her brow as she writes, I fear she is filling the pages with anxieties and troubled thoughts.

But then without warning another Alexandra appears — one who is filled with restless energy, who talks too quickly, too obsessively, who never sleeps.

This morning she looked up from her well-worn copy of the *Bhagavad Gita.* "Tell me, Jeanne, why should I study? Am I hoping to impress everyone with my superior knowledge? I don't wish to become boring and ridiculous. Only think of M'sieu d'Artois!"

"Surely," I said, "one studies to acquire wisdom."

"Or is it merely to gain the good opinion of others? Besides, it is science one learns in the lecture hall, not wisdom. Wisdom is what I find in library of the Musée Guimet."

And then setting down her book and carefully marking the page, she said "You're right, of course. It will soon be autumn, and there are decisions I have to make. You know that my parents want me to marry, to live in Brussels, to become a respectable member of the bourgeoisie. I have an inheritance, which my parents wish me to invest in a tobacconist's shop. But in October I will be twenty-one, and answerable to no one but myself. I can use my money in any way I see fit." She gave me a bleak smile. "Yes, chère Jeanne, you need not remind me, an inheritance does not last forever. I know if I do not want a husband — as most assuredly I do not — then I should be thinking of a career."

As should both of us, I thought, but did not say it aloud. Instead I pointed out, "You've trained in music. You have a lovely voice."

"A career on the stage? Perhaps—but think what dedication that requires. On the other hand — can you see me as a shopkeeper?"

In truth, I could not.

"When I was a child," Alexandra said, "I had arranged my whole life in advance. I had such enthusiasm, such idealism — do you know that once I imagined I had a vocation in the Church?"

Now, after days of gloomy silence, a torrent of words spilled out. Once again there was passion and energy in her voice. "The life of the convent seemed like an intoxicating dream, full of light and incense and flowers. That was where I thought I could come nearest to approaching the infinite, the unknowable. And even now I tell myself that I should follow the true faith — the God of my childhood. But Jeanne," and I realized that she was looking at me with something close to despair, "Jeanne, I am drawn to so many beliefs, so many strange gods. I keep imagining that there is some ultimate hidden truth that I have yet to discover — that no road, however dangerous, must be left unexplored."

I knew that Alexandra's belief in God is nothing like my parents' quiet, unquestioning faith. For her, it is a great mystery, a part of the even greater mystery of her own existence: a source of endless curiosity, and endless struggle.

She once told me she was "born Catholic, raised Protestant, Buddhist by inclination!" One day, someone may write the story of her life, and how will they describe her? As an anarchist, a scholar, an adventurer? An initiate into the mysteries of religion — or the mysteries of the occult? Or will she simply disappear into history?

Once she left her journal lying open on her desk, and I confess, I could not help myself — I stole a guilty glance at the words she had just written.

I search, I find. I wish to catch a glimpse of the sublime, the perfect, and this vision is like a spectre which I pursue . . .

I remember on another occasion that she looked up from her writing, and with a wry smile read me what was on the page: *I have little taste for mediocre things—mediocre comfort, mediocre situations, and mediocre success.*

And the thought came to me, that Madame Blavatsky might well have written those words. In their disdain for the rules of the ordinary world, in their restless search for what lies "beyond", she and Alexandra are more alike than either one of them suspects.

It came to me also, why Alexandra seemed disturbed by M. Gustave Moreau's chimeras. Surely she must have recognized in them the very spectres that beckon her along this uncharted path.

For me, the inexplicable arrived unsought, unbidden. At best it made me embarrassed and ashamed. At its worst it terrified and overwhelmed me. Now I want to cry out to Alexandra, "Take care what you do, Alexandra! There are roads we are not meant to travel."

CHAPTER THIRTY-SIX

August 12

Yesterday a letter from Mr. Rufus Dodds brought Madame Blavatsky very much to mind.

Mr. Dodds told me of his historical research, which though going well, has convinced him there is no clear end in sight; and he described Madame Rulenska's latest excursions into the occult (she is now writing poems and painting pictures dictated by the spirit world, with very odd results). He ended with warm wishes for my good health, my good fortune, and my personal safety.

And then I saw there was a second page, with a cryptic postscript: *By the way, it would seem that some time soon you might receive an unexpected visit.*

Those few words at first glance made the blood drain from my face, my heart constrict. Were my worst fears realized? Could word of George's death have reached Paris? Was I to be visited by the police?

But as I looked back at the rest of Mr. Dodds's cheerful letter, there was no hint of so dire a possibility. I showed the letter to Alexandra. "A visitor, writes Mr. Dodds. But who would visit me? Who knows I am here?"

"The Countess Constance, perhaps? Or one of the Keightleys? I know you have kept in touch."

I shook my head. "They have good manners — they would not dream of simply arriving unannounced. And why does Mr. Dodds not say who it is?"

All at once it came to me. "But of course — it can only be Madame Blavatsky herself! She is already travelling in France, and only HPB would turn up without warning on one's doorstep. Indeed, she has been known to descend bag and baggage upon friends and mere acquaintances for a fortnight's stay. I expect Mr. Dodds has read somewhere that she is on her way to Paris, and is speaking half in jest."

Alexandra looked stricken. "Clearly, she cannot descend upon *us* for a fortnight."

"Of course she will not," I said. "We are very fortunate that we have only two rooms between us, and not a villa. Mr. Dodds may simply be having his little joke. But just in case, we had best lay in a stock of coffee and good English biscuits."

Truth to tell, I do not really mind the thought of a visit from HPB. It might serve to distract Alexandra from the anxieties and obsessions that beset her.

CHAPTER THIRTY-SEVEN

August 16

I am frightened for Alexandra. Each day she seems more overwhelmed by a nameless and inexplicable grief. Melancholia, neurasthenia — whatever name a physician might use, it has descended like a black shadow blotting out the sun. What has become of my high-spirited companion, with her fierce appetite for life? Now all of Paris lies before her like a gift, and she turns her face away. Her talk is no longer of philosophy and eastern wisdom; instead she speaks of self-doubt and loss of faith. Hour upon hour she sits at her desk in that stifling and oppressive room, writing what she says are her "confessions" — as martyred to tormenting thoughts as a mediaeval saint.

Today when I went to her room she set down her pen and turned to me with troubled eyes. "What do you think happens to us when we die, Jeanne? Do you believe there is eternal bliss — or is there nothingness . . . annihilation?"

Her question startled and distressed me. This is a subject I try my best not to think about. "I was taught that our souls rise to heaven," I replied.

"But who can possibly know? What if our souls are reborn on earth, and then we are doomed to struggle and suffer all over again? That is what Buddhists believe, and their only hope is to achieve Nirvana — a sort of eternal nothingness. Nirvana is what I would wish for myself, Jeanne, if only I had the choice."

I wanted to weep for the dull weight of hopelessness in her voice. And then she went on: "If I knew that with one bullet I could scatter all the atoms of my body, could forever extinguish my spirit — but how can I be sure of that? God might see me as a soldier who has deserted her post, and then I would be punished for all eternity."

"Alexandra, please, I beg you, stop!" I clapped my hands over my ears, for I could not bear to listen to this wild talk. I have grown all too familiar with death and disembodied spirits and souls who return to walk the earth. They are spectres I hoped, finally, to have escaped.

I have learned to accept an Alexandra who consorts with anarchists and dissolute poets, who drinks absinthe, smokes cigarettes and is known to the police. But this new Alexandra, with all the light and joy vanished from her eyes, who talks of bullets, and annihilation, and death as something to be freely chosen, is one that I can scarcely recognize.

August 18

There has been no sign of the threatened visit from Madame Blavatsky. At this moment I would half-welcome her ill-tempered, obstreperous presence. For all her eccentricities, HPB has a large measure of common sense, and I desperately need to share my concerns about Alexandra.

August 20

Today I went to Alexandra's room thinking to borrow a new nib for my pen, but when I knocked there was no answer, and so I opened the door and went in. I knew she kept her writing materials in a chest of drawers, and would not mind if I helped myself. I opened a top drawer, found gloves and handkerchiefs, so tried another lower down. I lifted out some envelopes and a notepad, hoping to find the package of nibs lying underneath.

What I found instead was a pistol and a box of bullets.

CHAPTER THIRTY-EIGHT

August 21

Yesterday's discovery has filled me with a cold, sick dismay. How can I leave Alexandra alone for even a moment? For weeks now I have known that something was terribly amiss; yet until I caught sight of what was hidden in that dresser drawer, I had not let myself believe that she was in mortal danger.

During the day I will do my best to stay close by her side — but what of the night, when the darkest and most dangerous thoughts are entertained? I have settled on a pretext, flimsy though it may be, to keep watch by night as well.

This morning I told Alexandra, "My room is so hot and close I can scarcely get any sleep. The window is stuck fast, and no effort of mine will dislodge it. M'sieu Jourdan has promised to fix it, in his own good time — but I can only imagine when that may be."

Alexandra had a book propped open beside her plate, and was holding a cup of coffee long since gone cold. She seemed only to be half-listening to my complaint; but after a moment she looked up and said, "Chérie, you had but to ask, of course till it is fixed you must stay with me."

And so it is arranged that tonight I will move into Alexandra's room.

August 22

My sleep last night, in Alexandra's narrow bed, was broken and uneasy. For a long time I lay in a half-doze while she tossed and turned beside me. Eventually I must have slept, but some time after midnight Alexandra suddenly cried out, startling me awake. She sat up in bed and began to talk in such a rambling, disconnected way that I guessed she must still be dreaming. There were words in French — *démon, forêt* — and others that might have been some eastern language, Sanskrit, or Tibetan perhaps, all jumbled together and spoken in a frightened murmur.

I seized her by the arms and tried, as gently as I could, to shake her awake. Slowly the dazed, blank look in her eyes gave way to consciousness. Though the room was uncomfortably warm, her teeth began to chatter. When I put my arms around her shoulders to quiet her trembling, I was shocked to feel how thin she had become.

"Alexandra, you're awake now, it's all right, you've had a nightmare."

"*C'est la peinture,*" she whispered. Still seeming half in delirium, she spoke those words with a strange fascination, and wonderment, and dread. *"C'est la peinture . . . "* A long shudder ran through her, and then she lay back on the pillow with an exhausted sigh.

August — ?

I am sure of nothing: neither of the date, nor of the season, nor of the natural laws that govern the world, which I once thought immutable. But I have promised myself that I would make this journal an honest record, even of events that are impossible for me to comprehend, and still less possible to explain. I have delayed too long, trying to find words to describe the indescribable.

On the night of which I write, Alexandra was still running a slight fever and seemed in no better spirits; and so, as had been our habit for a while, we stayed in and retired early. I had been asleep for perhaps an hour or two, when I woke to find myself alone in the bed.

Seized with a fearful suspicion, I called out, "Alexandra!"

There was no answer. I got up, fumbled for matches, lit the bedside lamp. The room was empty.

And then — guided, perhaps, by some instinct arising out of panic—I noticed the book that Alexandra had left on her nightstand with a folded paper marking her place. I picked it up. *Sagesse,* it was called — Wisdom. A book of poems by Paul Verlaine. I opened it to the page she had been reading. Verlaine's despairing verses filled me with such foreboding that I can still see every word as though inscribed in the air.

A deep black sleep
falls upon my life:
sleep, all hope,
sleep, all desire . . .

and then the final stanzas*:*

I see nothing,
I have lost the memory
of evil and of good . . .
Oh, sad history!
I am a cradle
which a hand balances
in the hollow of a sepulchre.
Silence, silence.

Surely it was no accident, I thought, that she had left that poem for me to find. But what message did she intend? My heart raced with fear and a terrible confusion.

A deep black sleep falls upon my life . . . Silence, silence. "If I knew," Alexandra had said, "that with one bullet I could scatter the atoms of my body . . . "

I went to the chest, pulled out the drawer where I had found the pistol. To my immense relief it was still there, along with the box of bullets.

But suddenly I imagined Alexandra standing on a Paris bridge, about to throw herself into the waters of the Seine. I knew that somehow I must find her, must prevent whatever disastrous and misguided plan she had conceived — but where, in all this dark, sleeping city, should I begin to look?

Then I unfolded the sheet of paper that served for a bookmark and I read what was written there, in Alexandra's small, neat hand:

In a street, in the heart of a city of dreams,

that seems like a place where you have already been . . .

Her favourite lines of all Verlaine's work — so Alexandra had said, that night in the artist Gautier's studio. The city of dreams. The *Inconnu*. That place, both familiar and unknown, called "Elsewhere".

It was not death she would seek. Not Alexandra, who had valued life so dearly; who feared what terrible judgment might follow if like a faithless soldier she deserted her post. But to reach out for the mysterious, the unknowable — to venture on the dangerous road not yet explored . . . I remembered the words that Paul Verlaine had called after us, as we left M. Gautier's studio. "You and I, we could search together, Mademoiselle David. My good friend Gautier will know where to find me."

CHAPTER THIRTY-NINE

I was sick with apprehension as I tiptoed through the Jourdan's dining room and antechamber, then down the long flight of stairs to the street. At that hour the Boulevard St-Michel was still busy and I had no trouble finding a cab, though I could ill afford the expense. I gave the driver the address of M. Gautier's studio, and we set off for Montmartre.

I asked the cab to wait while I climbed the stairs to M. Gautier's studio. The artist was a long while coming to the door, but I could see a light through the transom and heard him moving about. Presently the door swung open, and M. Gautier appeared in carpet slippers, with collar undone and shirt-tails out. Behind him on the table stood an empty wine bottle and a single glass.

"Mademoiselle, how may I be of service?" he inquired with drunken formality.

I stepped inside without waiting for an invitation. "Have you seen my friend, Mademoiselle David? By chance did she come here, asking after M'sieu Verlaine?"

"Ah yes . . . " He gazed at me in cheerful befuddlement. "A pity, mademoiselle — I fear you have missed her. I offered her a glass of wine, but she would not stay. And true enough, she said she must find M'sieu Verlaine." He made an effort to tuck in his shirt. "But you, mademoiselle . . . you will have a glass of wine? There is another bottle somewhere, I think."

"Thank you, no . . . " I could scarcely conceal my impatience. "I cannot stay, I must find my friend. Please tell me, did you give her M'sieu Verlaine's address?"

"His address?" He laughed aloud at that. "Any cheap café in Paris — that is M'sieu Verlaine's address, mademoiselle. But tonight I know where you may find him, and I think also your friend. There is a gathering of artists at an apartment in the Latin Quarter." He fumbled for a pen and a scrap of paper, and scribbled down an address on the Boulevard du Montparnasse.

And so I had travelled across Paris, to learn that I might find Alexandra only a few steps from home, on the boulevard that crosses St-Michel. By now it was clearly too late for a respectable young woman to be out alone. My resolve was quickly fading. How easy it would be to retreat to the safety of my own room, with *chez Jourdan* close at hand. But I knew I must not turn back.

The concierge, seeming unsurprised by my arrival at this late hour, let me in to the building on the Boulevard du Montparnasse and directed me to the second floor. I walked up the carpeted stairs, thinking how foolish I would look if Alexandra were not here.

The servant who answered the door — if indeed he was a servant — was wearing a kind of Moorish costume with pantaloons and a sash. Glancing past him into the antechamber, I saw that it was surprisingly large and well appointed, with tapestries on the wall, and lamps in gilded sconces. I suppose I had expected another artist's garret like M. Gautier's, and now I felt even more uncertain. Summoning up what remained of my courage, I told him, "I have come to look for a friend."

"But mademoiselle, you must have mistaken the address, this is a private meeting." I was about to show him my scrap of paper with the address when a second man, still more exotically costumed, overheard and came to my rescue by inquiring the name of my friend..

"Ah yes, of course, Mademoiselle David. Please come in." I followed him through the antechamber and into a large drawing room where a number of people were gathered. I had a quick impression of a great many candles alight on lacquered Chinese chests, oriental-patterned wallpaper, Indian rugs and Japanese screens, a divan covered with a tiger skin. An incense burner emitted a strong odour of sandalwood, which could not disguise the smell of hashish cigarettes.

There, to my vast relief, was Alexandra. There also was M. Paul Verlaine.

By now I was feeling almost as angry as I was relieved. After all my alarm on her behalf, after my anxious pursuit through the streets of Paris, here she was, engaged in nothing more dangerous than a costume soirée.

Alexandra, glancing up, had seen me arrive. She gave me a look halfway between puzzlement and chagrin, and gestured to the empty place beside her. "Jeanne, *quelle surprise!* Do sit down. Why do you look so distressed?"

"Why should I not be distressed?" Had I ever before spoken so sharply to Alexandra? "I woke and you were not there. Who knew where you might have gone, or why?" I felt my throat tighten, my eyes begin to sting.

"But chérie, you found me, did you not? As you see, I did not go far. And you have come at just the right time. The entertainment is about to begin."

It was weeks since I had seen her in such high spirits. I should have been delighted. Instead I wanted to burst into tears.

Still, I was here and had accomplished my purpose. Alexandra was safe. As Alexandra was fond of saying, you should never refuse a chance for adventure. And so I drew some deep breaths, and felt a little better.

Looking around, I realized that nearly everyone was in costume. There were oriental potentates in long silk robes, Turkish pashas in embroidered vests, pale mediaeval ladies with mysterious smiles, and peacock feathers in their hair.

The man who presided over this peculiar gathering was dressed more austerely than the others, in a long white high-collared robe. Now, calling for everyone's attention and holding up a staff with a curving top like a shepherd's crook, he talked for a few minutes about the mystical artistic vision, and the magical power of words. After some persuasion M. Verlaine stood up and read one of his own poems, and one of M. Baudelaire's called "Les Metamorphoses du Vampire", from *Les Fleurs du Mal*. Afterwards we heard verses by Mallarme, Rimbaud and Mr. Edgar Allan Poe — all of whom seemed quite obsessed with dead flowers, drowned maidens, vampires and sarcophagi. Many of the poems were dark and disturbing. Some of them — in particular the one by the notorious Arthur Rimbaud (now said to be a gun-runner in Abyssinia) — were so shocking that I wondered if, with my still imperfect French, I had mistaken their meaning.

These people in their oriental finery, with their clever talk of art and literature and music, were surely no more odd than others I had met in Paris — the anarchists, the artists, the very peculiar M. d'Artois. And yet I felt a vague but growing unease.

"It is a little like Madame Blavatsky's dinner parties, is it not," I whispered to Alexandra.

"Except for the costumes, of course. And even HPB would have blushed at M'sieu Rimbaud's poem."

Alexandra smiled at that, but I could see that her mind was elsewhere. Her face was flushed; she had a feverish, over-excited look that I had seen before, and it made me anxious for her.

"Now," said our host, "for the surprise of the evening. I have recently acquired a most remarkable painting, by a young artist possessing a unique and astonishing talent. His is a mystical art imbued with a dark and inexplicable magic; art that transcends all that we understand of everyday reality. Join me, if you will, in experiencing the unimagined."

Obediently we followed him into an adjoining room, a sort of *salon des artes*, empty of furniture save for some tall oriental vases and, in one corner, an alcove upon which stood a carved Hindu deity.

On three of the walls were some Japanese prints, a painting of a woman in a field of poppies, and what Alexandra told me was a collection of Byzantine Madonnas. Most of the fourth wall was occupied by a large landscape painting.

It was in front of this work that everyone had gathered, with an air of excited curiosity.

C'est très mystérieux," they murmured. *"C'est très extraordinaire."*

It seemed to me an accomplished but unexceptional painting of wasteland, scattered shrubbery and distant mountains. Puzzled, I moved closer to examine it.

Then someone asked, "Who is the artist?" and someone else replied, "I believe it is the work of M'sieu Jacques Villemain."

And all at once I understood.

Once, many months ago, Alexandra had spoken to me of just such a painting — at first glance an unremarkable landscape of deserted heath, and lake, and snowcapped peaks. And then with a shiver of fear she had described the phantom images she had seen glimmering at the edge of vision — the mocking, demonic faces that were part of the landscape and at the same time — *something else.*

Still haunted by that vision, Alexandra had cried out in her sleep, "*la peinture.*"

Now, superimposed upon M. Villemain's deceptively innocent painting, I saw for myself those same malevolent shapes that had frightened Alexandra: the things that might have been human, or animal, *or something else.*

Perhaps the other guests had sensed the danger in the painting: as though by agreement, they had moved back to view it from a safer distance.

All except for Alexandra.

I wanted to shout out to her M. Villemain's warning: venture too close and the painting could take you captive. Step over the borders of the world into that perilous landscape, and there might be no escape.

Instead I moved to her side and whispered, "Alexandra, don't do this, you know it is dangerous."

But when had Alexandra ever turned away from danger? There at the very threshold of the Beyond, the *Inconnu*, she stood in a waking trance. Her breath had become so faint that I could scarcely detect any movement of her bosom. And then she put out a hand, and gently but deliberately, touched the surface of the painting.

CHAPTER FORTY

When Alexandra spoke of the Beyond, that other plane of existence so dangerously near our own — when she talked of astral counterparts and the Immaterial Realm — I had listened, and thought I understood. And yet I had not truly believed. Those experiences must be waking dreams, I thought, or opium-induced hallucinations. For better or worse, I could no longer deny my own wild talent; but this talk of astral travel put me too much in mind of Madame Rulenska's fraudulent spirits, or the Theosophists' fanciful beliefs.

Alexandra's hand had fallen limply to her side. Her eyes were open, but when I spoke to her she did not answer; nor did she seem aware of anything around her. After a moment someone brought a chair and when I placed a hand on her shoulder, she not so much sat down as subsided into it. It seemed she was sinking ever more deeply into unconsciousness.

Earlier, I had seen her drinking wine, and smoking a hashish cigarette. Surely, I told myself, this was the explanation: there was no magic here; she had merely fallen into a faint.

But then I glanced up at the painting, and my breath caught in my throat. There at the very edge of the canvas — where a moment before there had been nothing, only an empty stretch of wasteland — a small dark-clad figure had suddenly appeared, as though painted by an invisible hand.

The Alexandra of this world slept on, oblivious to that other self now setting out into uncharted country. But where was M. Verlaine, who should have accompanied her? I turned to see him staring at the painting. On his ravaged face was a look of anguish, and I guessed that in the end his courage, like his disease-ridden flesh, had failed him. His city of dreams, that he had sought so long to discover, must remain beyond his reach. He could only watch in despair as Alexandra went alone into the *Inconnu*.

But who would be her companion on that strange and hazardous journey? Who would bring her safely back? I could not abandon her, as Verlaine had done.

I stretched out my hand and felt the rough texture of M. Villemain's painting beneath my palm. Like the woman in the Paris drawing room who had found herself in the place she called "Elsewhere", like the woman who had wandered into an African landscape and left her handkerchief under a palm, I discovered how terrifyingly easy it can be to stumble over the edge of the known world.

Was it the "superabundance of psychic energy" that Alexandra had once told me I possessed, the same energy that had cursed me with my wild talent? Was it my frantic state of mind as I sought Alexandra through the dark Paris streets; or was it only the effect of hashish smoke and incense and overexcitement in that close hot room?

It took no more than a moment. I felt my vision blurring, my hearing muffled as though my ears were stuffed with cotton wool. I could not move. And then I felt a steady, insistent pull, that I knew was beyond my power to resist. So must a swimmer feel, caught up in an undertow and drawn helplessly out to sea. For an instant I saw myself — my other self, my spirit twin — as a vague shape rapidly fading into distance, and between us, thinning as it lengthened, a silvery, hazy cord.

THE BEYOND

*To pursue the mysteries on our earth is not
without danger, but how much greater the risk
incurred by those whose imagination incites
them to wander in those domains they believe
are situated beyond our normal frontiers.*

— Alexandra David-Néel,
Le sortilège du mystère

W hat I noticed first was the strangeness of the light — a shimmering luminescence that had the deceptive, distorting quality of moonlight. I had a sense of unseen presences — things that lurked in shadow, just beyond my vision. I could not pause to marvel at this place in which, inexplicably, I found myself; nor did I have time to be frightened. Some distance off I could see Alexandra's small, determined figure moving across the heath. I called out her name, and gathering up my skirt I raced after her.

She turned and caught sight of me. "Jeanne!" she cried out in dismay. "What have you done? I never meant you to follow me!"

"I know." I was too hot and out of breath to explain, or to argue. "But I followed you all over Paris, and a fine chase you led me. And now I am here. And you must make the best of it."

At that she smiled, and threw up her hands in a very Parisian shrug, and reached out to embrace me. *"Ma chère* Jeanne," she said. "What a foolish thing you have done! You know that I never meant to lead you into danger — but how glad I am that you are here!"

She gestured across the heath to distant mauve-coloured peaks, half-shrouded in mist and crowned with snow. Her eyes alight with excitement, she said "There is where I mean to go."

But I had already guessed our destination. Alexandra had always talked of finding her destiny in the mountains, in the high unvisited places of the world.

"And that is where this journey ends?" I asked.

"It is where the painting ends," she said. I thought I heard a hesitation, a faint note of uncertainty in her voice, and I felt a chill, but it was too late to turn back, and so I walked with her in silence over the trackless ground.

"The trick is not to glance sidelong," warned Alexandra; but in spite of myself I let my gaze wander towards the spiny thickets that grew here and there across the plain. I saw them, as I feared I would — those crouching, misshapen things that were neither animal nor human. Their sly, malicious faces wavered and dissolved like ghosts called up in a séance. Their malevolence, their mindless ill-intent, hung in the air like a foul smell.

By the time we reached the edge of the heath the sun was low on the horizon. Soon it slipped behind the peaks, and a brassy sunset, purplish-red and amethyst and saffron, spread across the sky. Bruise-coloured shadows gathered as we moved through the grey gloom. Presently we came to the reedy margins of a lake — the half-glimpsed lake of M. Villemain's painting. Mists writhed like serpents over the dark, oily water.

Footsore and exhausted, we knew we could go no further. Strangely we felt neither thirst nor hunger, only an aching heaviness of body and spirit. We lay down together on the sparse grass beside the lake, and eventually drifted into sleep. Once I woke in the black of the moonless night and thought I saw huge glowing faces, like silver masks, floating over the surface of the water. Trembling, I moved closer to Alexandra for comfort; but then I persuaded myself it was only a dream, and I fell back into uneasy slumber.

At dawn we set out along the lakeshore. Distances, like the light, were deceptive here, and it was afternoon by the time we reached the farther side. We made our way across an almost featureless ash-coloured plain, and came at last to bleak wind-scoured slopes, made treacherous by shifting scree. I followed Alexandra into the mouth of a gully, which grew narrow and deeper as it ascended, with grey, moss-streaked crags rising sheer on either side.

The sky was a thin streak of silvery blue far overhead; scarcely any light reached the floor of the ravine. For what seemed like hours we clambered in near-darkness over boulders and rotting logs.

The root-buttressed path grew steeper, and the gully gradually shallower, until we were once again on the bare mountainside. We came over a ridge between two peaks, and found that we had reached the top of a pass. Sprcad out below us was the shadowy, uncharted country that lay on the far side of M. Villemain's mountains. We had travelled beyond the edges of the canvas, into an elsewhere that perhaps the artist had not yet imagined; and now I felt real fear.

"Alexandra, it's time to turn back."

I had seen the exhilaration, the eagerness in her face as she gazed across that mapless landscape, and I knew well enough how she would reply.

"But to leave off now in the midst of such an adventure . . . *quel dommage*!"

"But be sensible, Alexandra! You said this is where the adventure would end. If we go farther, surely every step will lead us into danger — and how shall we find our way home?"

"And yet . . . " She was gazing into the far distance, where other higher mountains loomed against the darkening sky. Then she turned and looked back at the way we had come.

As I bent to tighten a bootlace, I heard Alexandra's sharp cry of dismay. I straightened and whirled round.

The path through the ravine that would lead us back down the mountain had vanished. The ravine itself, and the surrounding slopes, had ceased to exist. We were standing on the edge of a precipice, and below us was a black chasm, filled with swirling tendrils of mist

There *was* no way back.

CHAPTER FORTY-TWO

I n that that first moment, as I looked down into the abyss, I was too panic-stricken to speak. When Alexandra turned to face me I saw shock and confusion in her eyes, and a fear as great as my own.

In the midst of my terror I felt a sudden rush of anger — perhaps more at myself than at Alexandra. Why, when I understood the danger, had I followed her without a second thought?

Alexandra moved away from the cliff-edge and came to put her arms around me, as though seeking comfort, or forgiveness. She pressed her cold cheek to mine. "Jeanne, truly I am *désolé!* This was a journey I was meant to take alone."

I found my voice. "But with no way to return?"

"How could I have known? Others have come back safely."

But had she known, would she have turned back, I wondered? These past weeks she had seemed so wrongheaded, so heedless of danger.

She drew away then, and pointed towards the horizon. "Look over there, Jeanne. Are those not the spires of a city? And more mountains beyond?"

I followed her gaze. The valley beneath us was now lost in mist and shadow. But in the far distance dark towers rose, and behind them mountain ramparts, a black wall against the sky.

We could scarcely remain where we were. There was no choice but to go on.

It might have been dawn, or midday, or evening. As we wound our way down a narrow path into the valley I realized we had lost all sense of time. The sunless sky was the colour of pewter. Everything was bathed in a halflight that leached all the colour from the rocks, from the stony earth with its patches of lichen and dead grass, from the leafless, scraggly trees.

Presently we came to flat, marshy ground surrounding a stagnant pool overgrown with weeds. The air was rank with the stench of rotting vegetation. Hanging from the gnarled limbs of willow trees were what looked at first glance like pale round fruit; but when we drew closer we saw to our horror that they were human skulls. Roots snaked up through the dank earth, entwined with other bones. A bird with the head of a rat swooped past us; small scaled creatures scuttled among broken ribcages that shone with the phosphorescence of decay.

My teeth began to chatter. "Surely this is not how you imagined it, Alexandra — the Beyond, the *Inconnu?*"

"I did not know how to imagine it. But never like this."

I search, I find. I wish to catch a glimpse of the sublime, the perfect . . . I recalled with bitter irony those passionate lines in Alexandra's journal. What a cruel joke — to go in search of the perfect and sublime, and find instead the country we visit in our darkest nightmares.

《 《 《

What words can convey the strangeness of our journey? The landscape through which we now travelled might well have been some desert place on earth — a flat dun-coloured wasteland crossed here and there with gullies and littered with broken stone. The low sky had darkened to a leaden grey; the air was close and heavy, with no breath of wind. But how to write of stunted trees with forked trunks that rattled their skeletal limbs as we passed, shrieking in distress? Or fields of leprous flowers, their thick, fleshy petals oozing blood?

And how shall I describe the creatures we encountered, part beast, part human, as grotesque as any portrayed in M. Moreau's painting? From a tumble of rocks a crouching sphinx with a woman's face regarded us with her flat unblinking gaze. A basilisk slithered across our path, its breath scorching the dry earth, its eyes like burning coals. Most frightening of all was a huge beast with a crimson lion's body and a human face, its jaws crowded with glittering rows of fangs. Catching sight of us he reared on his hind legs and that fearsome mouth yawned open — only to fill the air with a sweet, enticing music of pipes and trumpets.

"Don't listen," cried Alexandra. "That creature is a manticore, and he has a taste for human flesh." Pursued by that eerie, seductive music, we hurried on.

The paintings I had seen these past months in Paris were filled with disturbing, otherworldly visions; the poems I had heard seemed inspired by fever dreams or opium. Those artists, those poets, surely had explored this same hallucinatory landscape, and had returned to record their visions.

But some, I think, it had driven mad. I trudged after Alexandra, who forged onward with her usual stubborn resolution, never losing sight of the far-off city and the mountains beyond — and I wondered, was that the fate awaiting us?

CHAPTER FORTY-THREE

A long the sides of the valley stood a row of statues carved from immense blocks of black stone. Those silent presences, with their hollow, staring eye sockets, seemed as menacing as anything we had yet encountered.

This place, now, was our reality; the Paris drawing room where my other self lay senseless in her chair had faded to a dream.

As we went on the landscape altered, became green and lush; the air was rich with flowery scents. Trees arched overhead, dripping with wisteria and tropical vines. Rank jungle vegetation crept across the path. Then the land rose sharply, and as we crested a rise, Alexandra, walking a little ahead, gave a cry of astonished joy.

There in the near distance rose a city of out of fairytale. Slender white spires glittered against a sky no longer grey, but azure. As we approached, the city revealed itself in a gorgeous confusion of turrets and cupolas and campaniles, gilded domes and steeples, jeweled mosaic walls and gates of shining metal. Could this be some fabled city of antiquity — Byzantium, or Samarkand , or Xanadu?

"The city of dreams," breathed Alexandra, breaking our awestruck silence.

"Poor M'sieu Verlaine," I said. "How sad that he will never see it."

We passed through gates of gilded bronze and climbed a flight of marble stairs. At the top was a pillared colonnade lit by hanging lamps of silver filigree. It opened onto a broad plaza lined on both sides by arcades, their columns and archways sheathed in mother-of-pearl. The floor was paved (marvelled Alexandra) with sardonyx and malachite and rose-quartz. But there were no shops or cafés or market booths, no musicians or chestnut sellers or children playing. We saw no one, heard not a single human voice.

We held our breath, not daring to look away for an instant, for fear this miraculous city would vanish, as the road behind us had vanished, and we would find ourselves once again on the edge of an abyss. And so we stood for a long while gazing at tapestries embroidered with gold thread and stitched with pearls; rows of alabaster statues; wall panels of delicate green and silver cloisonné; waterlilies like scraps of moonlight floating on a lapis lazuli pool.

And yet, there was wrongness here. It was like a faint whiff of mildew and decay, not quite disguised by the fragrance of sandalwood and jasmine, an effluvium that somehow seeped from the iridescent columns, the gleaming marquetry.

And where were the people who should have inhabited this enchanted place?

At the end of the plaza was an archway set in a wall of ice-white crystal. I looked at Alexandra, saw my own fearful uncertainty reflected in her face. What lay beyond? Would we discover palaces and pleasure-gardens? Lords and ladies in cloth-of-gold and peacock feather masks? Or would we find only hushed and echoing courtyards, deserted streets?

There was another question neither of us wished to ask aloud. Beyond that glimmering archway, would we find our way home?

We stepped through. And everything changed.

We looked out across a dismal ash-grey cityscape, an endless vista of black columns and featureless granite walls. A bitter wind scattered dead leaves along the cobbled street, chased dark clouds across a waning moon.

At first we heard only voices: a thin, wordless chorus of lamentation, a sound filled with such inexpressible misery that we wanted to stop our ears. And then we saw what had made those cries. They were everywhere, circling all about us: faceless things made of dusk and shadow, ribbons of blackness swirling around the basalt pillars, scarves of smoke blown across the cobbles and congealing into clots of darkness. Now and again there was the suggestion of a blind dead eye, a skeletal limb, a mouth gaping in a howl of fury or despair.

And I knew them at once for what they were.

"... *I have seen a monstrous bodiless creature seizing hold of someone. It wraps itself around its victim like a black shroud, and slowly disappears as if drawn into his body through his living pores.*" Thus Madame Blavatsky had spoken of disembodied spirits, soulless re-animated shadows desperate to regain a human form. I saw Alexandra cross herself, saw her lips move in a silent, terror-stricken appeal to her childhood God, and I knew that she remembered those words as well as I.

A creature made of shadow was taking hideous shape. Eyes burned like coals in its cadaverous face. It was the face I had tried all these months to forget, the one that still haunted my dreams. How well I knew that mocking grin, though it was infinitely more vengeful and malevolent now than it had been in life.

It wraps itself around its victim like a black shroud, and slowly disappears as if drawn into his body through his living pores . . .

George had come for his revenge.

CHAPTER FORTY-FOUR

T *his is how horror feels,* I thought: *horror is to have your flesh crawl, icy hands clutch your spine, your mind cringe away and shrink in upon itself, recoiling in disbelief.*

It was their relentless greed that gave these soulless shadow-things their power — their singleminded lust to inhabit a human form. This would be George's vengeance — that in the end he should possess not only my body, but my soul.

I could hear the murmur of Alexandra's voice, a quavering sound more chant than prayer, and no longer I think to our Christian God but to some eastern deity. Shuddering, half-fainting, my mouth filled with the bitter taste of bile, I thought, there are no gods that can save us now.

There was a time when I had power over George. It was not shame or disgust that had rescued me that long-ago day in the byre. It was a power born of rage and fear, of an instinct for self-preservation, a stubborn refusal to submit. I had not given in to George that day, for all that it was to cost me later. Whatever the price might be, I would not give in to him now.

When he was still solid flesh and blood I had managed to do him a grievous harm, though I had not meant to. How much easier now, I thought, to destroy this phantasm, held together by greed and blind desire and malice. I felt the familiar power rising in me, sweeping away my terror and guilt.

But then darkness wrapped itself around me, fell across my face in heavy, stifling folds. Something damp and loathsome pressed itself against my mouth and nose. I could not breathe, could not cry out. Under my clawing hands the stuff gave way like rotting cloth, yet still I could feel strands of it searching like fingers across my skin,

. . . *a black shroud . . . drawn in through the living pores . . .* As I clutched at my face and gasped for air, revulsion gave way to panic — and with panic came anger. Dimly I thought, *I do not deserve this.* I seized in both hands the thing that had once been George, the ghastly thing that still wished to possess me. In a fury I tore it from my flesh and ripped it into tattered shreds.

I was consumed, now, by my anger: a heart-pounding rage against what George had done, against what he had made me do—and what we had both become. It is a genie, this wild talent of mine, that I have learned to raise at will; but once released, I have no means by which to control it.

A great gust of wind shrieked across the cobbles, buffeted the granite walls, snatched up the last of the shadow-creatures and sent them howling into the night. There were sounds of rending and shattering, an immense ground-shaking roar as though a railway train were thundering overhead.

The pavement buckled under our feet. Grey dust, fragments of brick and stone, then heavier granite chunks rained down as walls and columns crumbled and collapsed around us.

Alexandra seized me by the arm and half-dragged me in a daze back through the archway into the plaza. But here too the destruction I had set in motion had begun. Cracks had begun to spread across the gleaming pavement. Gilt paint was flaking, strips of torn fabric hung from the tapestries; there were bare patches on the walls where the cloisonné had chipped and fallen away.

I was shuddering from shock and weakness — icy spasms that gripped me from head to foot. All I felt now was sadness, that I had destroyed not only what was evil in this place, but what was beautiful.

And in the Beyond that lies so near and yet so distant from our own, that was my last conscious thought.

❆ ❆ ❆

I remember a sense of weightlessness, of dissolution. I imagined myself as insubstantial as a wreath of smoke, adrift in some dark space between two worlds. And then I felt a painful, insistent tugging, as of a cord tightening. For an instant there was a horrible sensation that my spirit, or consciousness — my very soul, perhaps — was split in two, so that in some strange fashion I existed in two places at once.

And then, weak, dizzy, my stomach churning and my heart racing, I came to myself.

I was in the drawing room on the Boulevard du Montparnasse. There were people gathered around me, curious and concerned; and in the chair beside me, a bewildered Alexandra was waking from her own unnatural sleep.

Someone held a vial of smelling salts under my nose; a bearded man in Turkish costume, a doctor perhaps, was solemnly taking Alexandra's pulse.

"What time is it?" I murmured, emerging out of my daze. How heavy my limbs felt! I almost asked, "What day is it" — for it seemed that a vast amount of time had passed.

"Just gone eleven," someone said, consulting his pocket watch. "It seems that you young ladies have suffered a fainting spell. Fortunately it lasted for only a few minutes. There's no damage done, I expect."

Was that possible? In the world from which we had returned, did real time not exist?

With that thought, I glanced up at the painting. I saw that Alexandra's figure had vanished from the landscape, and though the canvas should have been ripped and shredded beyond repair, it seemed quite undamaged. "We've called for a cab," someone said. And someone else, a woman, said encouragingly: "A good night's sleep should set things aright."

I was grateful for their kindness, grateful too for how ordinary they all seemed, in spite of their costumes and their strange beliefs. I was grateful for the solid reality of this Paris drawing room. But life for me could never again be ordinary. Would I ever have a night's sleep that was not haunted by guilty dreams?

I had murdered George for a second time.

CHAPTER FORTY-FIVE

September 15

I have existed these weeks of early autumn in a kind of dream. I wander the streets and sit with Alexandra in the cafés of the *Rive Gauche*, and I try to plan for a future that seems no more real to me now than our wanderings in the Beyond.

In spite of all that has happened, Alexandra seems in excellent spirits. She has made up her mind to use her inheritance for travel in the Orient — first Ceylon, then India and the Himalayas. To that end she is working hard to improve her knowledge of Sanskrit and Tibetan. There are more than enough mysteries in our own world to be explored, she says.

But my own thoughts weigh heavily upon me. I realize now that in some corner of my mind I had clung to the possibility that George was still alive. But even that faint hope is shattered now.

And what havoc have I wrought, in the worlds above and beyond our own? Have I forever destroyed M. Verlaine's city of dreams?

Alexandra says no, and I try to take some comfort in her words. "This is what I think, *chère* Jeanne — that with every poem, every painting, a city of dreams is created, and so there are as many Elsewheres as there are artists who have dreamt of them."

I would like to think that M. Verlaine will someday find his magical city, but Alexandra says that a poet has only the courage of paper and pen, and that to travel in the Beyond you must be prepared to risk everything, perhaps even your life.

One smaller mystery puzzles us. What has become of the expected visit from Madame Blavatsky? By now we had thought to entertain that large and glowering presence. Secretly, I hoped to confess to her our adventures in the Otherworld. Though I knew she would call us something much worse than flapdoodles, I knew she would neither judge nor disbelieve us.

September 22

How suddenly life can change! Sometimes as I know to my cost it is disaster that unexpectedly descends, and alters everything for the worse. But sometimes, too, there can come an unlooked for, unimagined joy.

Our visitor has arrived.

CHAPTER FORTY-SIX

T he day had begun badly, with wind and driving rain. Alexandra, who never minds the weather, set off early to the reading room at the Musée Guimet, but I had decided to remain indoors.

I was in low spirits that morning and feeling all at loose ends. To occupy my time I began to sort through my few belongings and set my room to right. Tucked away in a drawer I found the very first of my journals, the one my mother had given me. I opened it and began to read, and my throat ached thinking of my family. I mourned as well my own innocent younger self, who wrote with the sound of the Borders on every page. Since then, I have filled a great many notebooks, and in this one, that I have just opened, I will write the last chapter of a story that is as strange as any by Mr. Walpole, or Mr. Poe.

I had just heated myself a cup of chocolate and was about to drink it in the Jourdan's chilly dining room when poor little Madame Jourdan crept in, and whispered that I had a visitor.

Madame Blavatsky, at last! I leaped to my feet all flustered, thinking how annoyed she would be, left standing in the narrow hallway. But had she come alone? How ever had she managed the stairs? And what could I offer her to eat, when I had just eaten the last pastry? All these thoughts were racing through my mind when outside in the hall a voice said, "*Merci, Madame.*"

It was the voice I longed most in the world to hear, and believed I would never hear again.

And then he was there in the doorway with rain in his hair, his face reddened by the wind and burned brown by the African sun. He said with a smile, "This is a fine chase you have led me, Jeannie Guthrie!"

"Tom," was all that I managed to say. "Tom . . . " And then my throat seized up, and my eyes stung, and I burst into tears.

《 《 《

Tom gazed at me across the dining table as though he feared I might try to escape. A pot of Earl Grey tea and a plate of biscuits sat forgotten between us. In my delighted astonishment I had almost scalded myself with the kettle.

"But you didn't expect me?" asked Tom, sounding puzzled. "Mr. Dodds said he would write and tell you I was coming to Paris."

"He only said I might have a visitor. I thought he meant Madame Blavatsky, because I knew she was travelling in France."

Tom laughed. "I hope I will be a less demanding guest. But Jeannie, what a trail I had to follow to find you! I was determined to see you again as soon as I returned from East Africa, but by then you had left Lansdowne Road and moved to Clerkenwell. And when you did not reply to my letter . . . "

"But Tom, I did reply!" I cried. "Of course I replied!" How could he imagine I had not? And then suddenly I remembered. When Tom's letter came, I had been too ill to leave the house. And I had left my answer to go out with the morning post.

"I watched all summer for a letter." There was regret in his voice, but no reproach.

"Oh, Tom, as did I!"

"And so I finally I went to Clerkenwell, and knocked on your door, and was informed by a rather disagreeable woman that you had run away to Paris."

"Madame Rulenska, Tom — that was Madame Rulenska." I could not help myself, the tears kept falling, the words came tumbling out. "She is a vile woman, and she told me your intentions were not honourable, and that I was a freak of nature, but Mr. Dodds said it was only because she needed my help with her tricks and illusions. And Tom, I know what happened. I left your letter to be posted, and Madame Rulenska must have taken it, and it was never sent."

"She looked like a woman entirely capable of such deception," Tom said. "But your Mr. Dodds — we are both of us in his debt. He told me you had gone to Paris, and gave me your address. Because there is a question I've come to ask you, Jeannie Guthrie."

He reached across the table, and from the way he took hold of my hand, as though he never meant to let it go, I knew what that question might be. And I knew, to my anguish, how I must answer.

He said, very solemnly — holding both of my hands now — "Jeannie Guthrie, I have come to ask if you will marry me."

And through my foolish tears I gasped out, "Tom, I cannot."

He seemed oddly undeterred by this reply. "Because you have a tendency to overturn tables, and fling things about the room? We all have our peculiarities, Jeannie — I dare say I have worse habits than that."

I shook my head. How could I possibly explain why I must refuse him? How could I tell him how truly wicked I was?

"I love your strangeness, your wild talent, Jeannie, just as I love your goodness and your courage. And now that I have spoken to Mr. Dodds, there need be no more secrets between us."

No more secrets? My heart flew into my throat.

"When Mr. Dodds saw that my intentions were honourable, and that I would not rest until I found you, he told me about your cousin. He confided to me what George had done — or tried to do — and that you believed you had killed him. An act of justified self-defense which would hardly have constituted murder — but still, that was what you believed, and then I understood why you sometimes had that haunted look, and would never talk about your past."

"And knowing that, you would still marry me? Tom, I have committed murder!"

"And for both our sakes, dearest Jeannie, I had to prove it was not so. If you remember, our friend Willie Wilde was let go by the *Telegraph*, and so he was glad of an opportunity to earn a little money with his journalistic expertise. I asked him to go to the Borders and see what information he could unearth."

For a moment I hardly dared to breathe.

"And happily, I can set your mind at rest. Whatever well-deserved damage you may have inflicted on George, it was hardly fatal. When you fled from the Borders George may have had a sore shoulder, but he was certainly not dead. Nor did he leave off assaulting innocent young women — not all of whom could defend themselves as well as you did. That was what Willie Wilde discovered, when he made discreet inquiries."

"But George *is* dead."

"Oh, to be sure. Now he is. If your mother had known where to write to you, you would have heard by now. George met a sordid end — but not by your hand."

"But how . . . ?"

"Let me finish the story. Willie made a search of the Berwick papers for death announcements, and sure enough, he found one for a George Guthrie, aged 20, drowned under mysterious circumstances. His body, it appears, was found floating in the Tweed. There was a Fatal Accident Inquiry by the Procurator Fiscal — I take it that's your Scottish version of a coroner — who in the end decided that it was just that, an accident. George had been seen drinking heavily in a public house, and so it was surmised that he had stumbled, lost his balance, and fallen in. The fathers and brothers of certain young women may have had further information, but they were never interviewed. And there the matter ends."

George dead — but not by my hand. I thought of the agonies of guilt I had suffered, the haunting dread that one day I would be discovered. I had paid dearly for that act of defiance.

"And now will you marry me, Jeannie Guthrie?"

I fumbled for my handkerchief. Tom smiled, and gave me his. I saw the kindness in his eyes, the steadfast love, and the determination.

This is my beloved, I thought, *and this is my friend.*

"Yes," I said. And that is the end of this story, and the beginning of another.

AUTHOR'S NOTE

It is not so much that so many poltergeist girls have been housemaids and "adopted daughters", as that so many of them have been not in their own homes; lost and helpless youngsters, under hard task-masters, in strange surroundings —

This quotation from Charles Fort may help to explain why a sensitive, studious young girl, uprooted from a loving home at the age of thirteen, and made to work long hours in the fields in all kinds of weather, might develop a wild talent.

On the farms of the Scottish Borders in the 19th century, field workers were mostly women and young girls. Hired or "bonded" at hiring fairs along with a male relative, they were known as bondagers, and they did every kind of heavy outdoor work except for ploughing.

In her London journal of 1888 Alexandra David mentions that she has engaged a young girl to help her practise speaking English. Though Alexandra says nothing further about this anonymous *jeune fille*, I have given her a name — Jeannie Guthrie — a history, and her own strange story to tell.

Many of Alexandra's early adventures in search of the *Inconnu* are recorded in journal entries published posthumously by Librairie Plon as *Le sortilège du mystère.* She has written in detail of her friendship with the artist Jacques

Villemain, and of his mysterious painting. As well, she describes the experience of an unnamed woman (quite probably Alexandra herself) who made a spirit journey to the astral plane, while connected to her physical body by a thin hazy cord. However, my imagined country of the Beyond springs not from Alexandra's writings, but from the visionary worlds of Symbolist artists.

In 1888 and 1889, Madame Helena Blavatsky, head of the British Theosophist movement, known to her friends and many admirers as HPB, was living in London's Holland Park. Fashionable and artistic London flocked to her Saturday afternoon salons. Alexandra's journal doesn't mention a visit to 17 Lansdowne Road, but given her fascination with the occult, we can be fairly certain that she was familiar with Madame Blavatsky's eccentric household.

I've been as faithful as possible to the recorded details of Alexandra's life in the years 1888-1889; as well as to the London career of Madame Blavatsky. For daily life at 17 Lansdowne Road I'm especially indebted *to Reminiscences of H.P. Blavatsky and The Secret Doctrine,* by Constance Wachtmeister et al (Theosophical Publishing House). However, the part that my fictional heroine Jeannie Guthrie might have played in their lives is pure invention

Soon after this story ends, Alexandra journeyed to India and Ceylon. When she returned to Paris, she became an opera singer, married, and then, with the financial help of her loyal and long-suffering husband, abandoned everything to become an explorer and a student of Buddhist mysticism. In the course of a very long and adventurous life, she travelled to the forbidden city of Lhasa, lived for two years as a hermit in a Himalayan cave, and wrote more than thirty books on Eastern religion and travel.

If you'd like to learn more:

Charles Fort, *Wild Talents* (Ace Books, 1932; reprinted in *Complete Books of Charles Fort,* Dover, 1975)

Barbara & Michael Foster, *Forbidden Journey — The Life of Alexandra David-Neel* (Harper & Row, 1987)

Philippe Jullian, *Dreamers of Decadence* (Praeger, 1971)

Ian MacDougall, *Bondagers: Eight Scots Women Farm Workers* (Tuckwell Press, 2000)

Marion Meade, *Madame Blavatsky, The Woman Behind the Myth* (G.P. Putnam's Sons, 1980)

Alexandra David-Néel, *My Journey to Lhasa* (Beacon Press, 1983)

EILEEN KERNAGHAN has worked in support of her writing as an elementary school teacher, arts administrator, used bookstore owner and, for many years, as a creative writing teacher at Shadbolt Centre for the Arts in Burnaby, and Port Moody's Kyle Centre.

Research for a non-fiction book on reincarnation inspired her first young adult fantasy, *Dance of the Snow Dragon*, set in 18th century Bhutan, and based on Tibetan Buddhist mythology. It was followed by *The Snow Queen*, which explored echoes of northern shamanism and the Kalevala in Hans Christian Andersen's classic tale. Her third YA fantasy, *The Alchemist's Daughter*, is set in Elizabethan England, a year before the Armada. *Winter on the Plain of Ghosts: a novel of Mohenjo-daro*, which also appeared in 2004, is a historical fantasy set in the ancient Indus Valley civilization.